Love Meant to Be

PREVIOUS BOOKS BY SALLY BAYLESS

The Abundance Series
Love at Sunset Lake
Love and Harmony
Love and Roses
Love Once More
Love of a Lifetime (prequel)
Christmas in Abundance (companion novella)

Love Meant to Be

THE ABUNDANCE SERIES BOOK 5

SALLY BAYLESS

KIMBERLIN BELLE PUBLISHING

Printed in the United States of America
First Printing, 2020
ISBN: 978-1-946034-14-4

Kimberlin Belle Publishing
Contact: admin@kimberlinbelle.com

Scriptures taken from the Holy Bible, New International Version®, NIV®. Copyright © 1973, 1978, 1984, 2011 by Biblica, Inc.™ Used by permission of Zondervan. All rights reserved worldwide. www.zondervan.com The "NIV" and "New International Version" are trademarks registered in the United States Patent and Trademark Office by Biblica, Inc.™

Publisher's Note: This is a work of fiction. Names, characters, places, and incidents are a product of the author's imagination. Locales and public names are sometimes used for atmospheric purposes. Any resemblance to actual people, living or dead, or to businesses, companies, events, institutions, or locales is completely coincidental.

Cover Design © Jennifer Zemanek/Seedlings Design Studio

Your love, LORD, reaches to the heavens, your faithfulness to the skies.
Psalm 36:5

Be kind and compassionate to one another, forgiving each other, just as in Christ God forgave you.

Ephesians 4:32

Chapter One

Meredith Lawson stepped onto her front porch and gazed up into the late afternoon sky.

Snowflakes poured down, as big and fluffy as popcorn. In less than an hour, her drab yard, leafless trees, and even the muddy field across the road had been transformed into a world of sparkling white.

She buttoned her old brown work coat, dug gloves out of the pockets, and tugged on her navy knit cap.

Duke, her German shepherd, raced off the porch and stuck his face in the snow, then lifted his head, black nose now frosted white. He let out a woof and bounded across the yard.

The vet might say Duke was a mature dog of nine, but he was still a puppy when it snowed.

Meredith pulled her phone out of the back pocket of her jeans, snapped a photo of Duke, and texted it to her sister, Ava, with the message "Happy New Year!"

Within seconds, her phone rang.

"Happy New Year to you as well!" Ava said. "Those flakes look enormous."

"They are."

"I'm so jealous." Ava let out a soft, pouty groan. "Here in Atlanta, it's rainy and gray. I wish I was still with you in Missouri."

"I wish you were too." Somehow, ever since Ava drove back to Georgia two days ago, things that Meredith hadn't noticed before stood out like lonely lighthouses in her life. The silence of the house at night. The meals alone in front of the TV. The fact that she ran her dishwasher half empty simply so bits of food wouldn't get dried onto the plates and silverware. Even sitting with her aunt and uncle at church this morning, she'd felt alone.

Still, she didn't want to discourage Ava from pursuing her dream at culinary school. Dreams were important. And speaking of dreams… "Even though you're missing the snow, I've got news that will brighten your day. If I can get a loan from the bank, I think I can make the plan for the restaurant work."

Ava squealed. "Really? You can buy Uncle Harris and Aunt Ruby's place?"

"I think so."

"Oh, sis, that would be amazing." Ava's words echoed with longing.

Meredith's heart warmed. It would be so wonderful to be able to do this for Ava. So fun for them to work as a team, with her growing organic produce in the greenhouse and Ava cooking it in her restaurant.

Of course, buying Ruby and Harris's place would

mean the loan would need to be sizable. And she wouldn't have much money left over each month after the payments. Certainly not enough for any exotic vacations. Not that she got away for vacations, with the greenhouse demanding all her time. But she and Ava had looked at rental space, and there was nothing at all suitable locally. Plus, buying her aunt and uncle's farmhouse next door wasn't just a good idea. It was the least she could do for Ava.

Plus, rejoining the properties made sense.

After all, the five acres she and Ava owned, along with the land where her aunt and uncle's house sat, had once been part of the same parcel, right outside the little town of Abundance. The property had only been divided after Grandma and Grandpa Carlton died when Meredith was five. They left Uncle Harris twenty acres, including the house, and left Mom twenty acres, plus their savings. Mom and Dad sold all but five acres and used the proceeds and the savings to build their own home and start the greenhouse business. Uncle Harris and Aunt Ruby stuck with traditional farming and, over the past three decades, had added six hundred acres to their land.

Meredith might find Uncle Harris difficult to be around, but she had to admit he was a good businessman.

Now that he and Aunt Ruby were retiring and moving south, if she could buy part of their land, the three acres with the house and yard, it would make a fabulous restaurant. Unlike the more modern, one-story ranch-style house her parents had built, the old Carlton family farmhouse had real historic charm. It was two and a half stories, built in the Queen Anne style, with a roomy wraparound porch and—best of all—a turret. Just the look of the place would attract customers from the city.

"Buying their house for the restaurant would be perfect." Ava sighed. "You could continue with the greenhouse, and once I finish culinary school, we could run the two businesses together. Farm to table, the ultimate in locally sourced food."

Meredith studied the big house next door. The more she played with the idea, the more she liked it. "I've been crunching the numbers all afternoon, and I think it will work. I just came outside to take a break because the snow is so pretty."

"If I was there, we could celebrate by building a snowman, like we always used to for the first real snow."

"We could. This snow is perfect. Wet enough to stick really well."

"You'll have to build it without me," Ava said. "Send me a picture."

Meredith pushed some snow back and forth with one foot. Building a snowman wouldn't be the same without her sister, but... "Okay. It's quite nice out here. Too nice to go right back inside." Besides, the beauty of the snow was exactly the kind of blessing she tried to take time to appreciate.

"I'll be waiting for the picture. And envisioning the menu for the restaurant. Thank you so much for trying this. I love you, sis."

"I love you too." Meredith hung up, tucked her phone back in her pocket, and scooped up a handful of snow. "C'mon, Duke, we've got a snowman to build."

Fifteen minutes later, the snowman was coming along well. Duke hadn't been nearly as much help as Ava, especially when it came to lifting the middle ball of snow on top of the bottom one. Still, Meredith had gotten the three snowballs stacked right in the middle of the yard where she and Ava had built their snowmen for years, ever since they were little, before Mom and Dad died.

Even during the four years that Ava had worked in a restaurant in Kansas City, she'd come home for her days off, for holidays, and for the first big snow. And next year, after Ava finished culinary school and moved back home, she and Meredith could continue their snowman-building tradition together.

Meredith brushed some snow away from the flowerbed by the front porch, gathered up a few pieces of mulch, and used them to create eyes and a cheerful smile.

Now she just needed Grandpa Carlton's fedora and a carrot for a nose.

"I'll be right back," she told Duke as she went inside.

Zach Gilcroft neared a curve on the narrow blacktop. He eyed the road, tightened his grip on the steering wheel of the rented Toyota, and carefully applied the brakes.

The car slid, its tires no match for the snow that had quickly piled to four inches.

He pressed more firmly on the brakes and, after a second, the anti-lock feature kicked in, putting him back in control of the vehicle.

Whew. He let out a silent breath, then glanced over at his thirteen-year-old daughter, Hailey, in the passenger seat.

Seatbelt on, long blond hair pushed back over her shoulders, she was smiling at her phone, oblivious to the road conditions. Probably thumbing through the photos she'd taken of that horse.

Kayla, the girl Hailey had met at church this morning, had been so nice to invite her over to see her horse. That one kind action had made such a difference. Most of the time they'd been here in Abundance visiting family for Christmas, Hailey had been just as unhappy as she had been back in Phoenix. Until she'd met Kayla.

Getting Hailey cheered up even for an afternoon was a big deal. So big that Zach had been reluctant to pull her away and had stayed, visiting with Kayla's parents, after he arrived to pick Hailey up. They probably should have left sooner.

Cautiously, he rounded the curve to where the road straightened.

Good thing he knew this stretch of County Road 1400 so well. He'd been out here in the snow many times as a teenager, driving Dad's pickup with a load of firewood in the back to make it easier to steer, when he visited a friend who'd lived a mile past Kayla's house. These days, though, at thirty-five, he was old enough to know to head home when the snow started to come down heavy.

Yet he'd lingered, foolishly hoping that one fun afternoon might somehow make up for the fact that Hailey was facing the evils of middle school without her mom to offer guidance.

Hailey set her phone on her lap. "Dad, do you think there's any way I could have a horse in Phoenix?" She looked over at him as if she didn't already know the answer was no.

A *no* that was hard for Zach to get out every time they

had this conversation. He loved his girl so much. Every day she reminded him more of her mom, with her big blue eyes and golden hair. If only Jillian were still alive to see their daughter growing up.

And to help him handle the murky waters of parenting a thirteen-year-old girl, a girl who had—after she seemed to recover from her mother's death—been so full of life. Until last year when she started middle school. Now, except for discussions about horses, Hailey was sullen and withdrawn.

"Buying a horse would be hard, princess." Zach caught her eye and shook his head. "With where we live, we'd have to board it, and I'm not sure how often you'd be able to get out to see it." He tried to keep his nights and weekends clear, but running his own energy business didn't allow nearly the amount of free time Hailey would want to spend with a horse.

"I bet we can find a stable close to town, and I can take the bus there after school to go riding."

Ride without him or another adult there to keep an eye on her?

That wasn't happening.

But somehow he had to find a way to get her past seventh grade. Truly, he was desperate enough to let the horse live in their garage and tell her she could ride it around their quarter-acre backyard in the suburbs and—

The car hit a slick spot and veered toward the right shoulder of the road.

Zach's pulse kicked up a notch, and Hailey sucked in an audible breath.

He steered into the skid, then eased the vehicle back

toward the center of his lane.

"How far"—Hailey's voice wobbled—"are we from Grandpa's place?"

"About three miles." He tried to sound confident. He'd like to give her a reassuring look as well, but after that skid, he didn't dare take his eyes off the road. "We just have these two big curves."

Curves that, even now, seventeen years after he'd graduated high school, still weren't banked right. He crept along, staying in the tracks from other cars as best he could.

Finally, he got back to another flat, straight part of the road. "We're in the home stretch now, Hailey. We have that little hill up ahead and after that we'll be on a road that's plowed."

"Good." She went back to her phone. "Although I'd rather be stuck in a ditch here than go back to Phoenix."

Her voice had that hopeless note again, the one that cut right into his heart. So much for cheering her up with a visit to a horse.

She let out a long sigh. "I can't believe I have to deal with Desert View Middle School again in only two more days."

Zach winced, gave the car a tiny bit of gas, and—

It fishtailed and spun out.

A thud sounded outside Meredith's house.

She put her gloves back on, grabbed the carrot and fedora, and opened the front door.

For a second she stood motionless, mouth open. The fedora and carrot fell from her hand, silently plunging into the snow on her porch.

There, in the middle of her front yard where her snowman had stood, was a light-blue sedan. The lower sections of her snowman were shattered. The snowman's head, fully intact, sat on the hood of the car with its smile still in place. And a tall, dark-haired man in a black jacket was climbing out of the car with his head angled to one side as if he couldn't quite take in what had happened.

Duke raced over, barking at top volume.

"Hush," she told the dog. "He's all bark," she called to the driver. "Really, a big love." She shut the front door and dashed over. "Are you hurt?"

"We're okay. I'd slowed almost to a crawl, but I couldn't stop before..." He gestured to the snowman's head on the hood of his car. "I'm afraid your friend sustained pretty serious injuries."

A young teenager climbed out of the car, hands covering her mouth, turquoise gloves the exact shade as her puffy coat. "Dad, you decapitated it!" A note of wrought-up emotion rang in her words, a note that tugged at something inside Meredith, reminding her of when Ava got upset when she was younger.

"Don't worry. I can fix it." Meredith lifted the snowman's head off the hood of the car and set it on the ground beside her. "I'm simply glad you're both okay. I'll build a new base for Mr. Snowman and do...well, a...a head transplant."

For a half-second the girl seemed unsure of how to react, then she gave a small smile.

Meredith grinned at her. Good, just like with Ava, a little humor helped.

The man walked closer and his scarf slipped down,

revealing a face with a strong jaw and familiar blue-gray eyes.

Eyes that sent a tingle through Meredith's chest.

"Thank you," he said. "For being understanding." His gaze held hers, as if adding unspoken thanks for how she'd lightened the mood.

But there was no glimmer of recognition in his eyes.

Maybe that was too much to expect.

"I'm sorry I ended up in your yard." He gestured to the muddy ruts behind the wheels of his car. "I'll be happy to pay to have new sod put down."

She brushed his offer aside. "Really, there's no need. I'll throw out some grass seed when it warms up."

"Are you sure? I feel like I should—" His eyes narrowed. "Wait a minute. I remember you. We went to school together. You're...Megan, isn't it?"

She pressed her lips together and mustered up a polite smile. "Meredith, Meredith Lawson. And you're Zach Gilcroft."

"Yeah." He tipped a head toward the girl. "This is Hailey, my daughter."

She'd heard he was married, living in some city out west, and was a pretty big deal. From the looks of things, it was true. She didn't know much about men's clothing, but those boots the girl was wearing cost $300.

So Zach was rich, married, and probably living a lifestyle she could only imagine. No wonder he barely remembered her. She was just plain old Meredith Lawson. Five foot four, fifteen pounds overweight, with brown hair and brown eyes. Whether it was when she'd had a crush on him at eighteen or today at age thirty-four, she was nothing memorable.

He opened his car door. "At least let me move my car and help with the, uh, head transplant."

"What? Oh, you don't need to—"

"I insist. The snow seems to have stopped, so the roads aren't getting any worse."

A minute later he'd backed the car into her driveway and begun rolling a snowball in the yard.

His daughter waited by the car, petting Duke.

Zach pointed to the place where the original snowman had stood. "Should we put him here?"

"Sure." She rolled her own snowball toward the spot. Zach's snowball was already larger. Clearly, it would be the base.

He angled his head toward the house. "I see those two big greenhouses out back. What do you grow?"

"Organic microgreens and a few bedding plants, especially flowers. What do you do?"

"I'm co-owner of a business in Phoenix in the energy sector, funded by venture capital."

That certainly sounded more impressive than growing baby radish and cabbage plants.

"We've been home for more than a week visiting family, but we fly back tomorrow." He smoothed the side of his snowball, flattening out a lump. "School starts in two days, and I need to get back in the office. It's pretty busy, being an entrepreneur and a single parent."

Meredith stopped rolling her snowball. "Single parent?"

"My wife died when Hailey was seven."

Oh. Poor Zach. Poor Hailey. Meredith glanced over at the girl, who was deep in conversation with Duke. It didn't

17

matter how old she was, a girl needed her mom. "I'm so sorry."

"It's okay," he said gently. "Here, let me." He took the second snowball from her, easily lifted it into place, and added the head. "Does that look good to you?"

"Even better than before. Thank you." She added branches for arms, then dashed to the porch, dug out the carrot and hat, brought them over, and positioned the carrot nose so that it pointed slightly up.

Zach took Grandpa's fedora and set it atop the snowman's head at a jaunty angle. Then he patted the snowman's shoulder. "Sorry about the incident, old fellow, but now you're as good as new." He turned to Meredith. "I guess we should get back on the road. If you're sure about the sod?"

"Seriously, do you know anyone in Abundance who puts down sod?"

He shrugged.

"Besides, I'm a farmer. If I can't get a little grass to grow, I need a different career."

He tipped his head in acknowledgment. "Then I guess we'll head back to my dad's place." He looked toward the car. "We should take off, Hailey."

The girl hugged Duke, waved, and got in.

Zach hesitated, then turned back to Meredith. "It's been nice seeing you." He caught hold of her hand, dwarfing her small navy glove with his big black one. "I miss people like you, living out in Phoenix."

A zing of warmth shot through her chest. "Have a good trip home." She stood there, waving, as he pulled onto the county road and drove away. The warmth in her chest fizzled out at the thought of how far away Arizona was.

There was no use getting excited over a chance encounter with Zach Gilcroft. He was out of her league. His time in Abundance was limited. He had big deals to put together in the energy sector.

And she had a loan to secure.

Chapter Two

"Thank you so much for seeing me, Ellen." Meredith sat down across from the loan officer and laid her black wool dress coat in the chair beside her.

Because New Year's Day fell on a Sunday, the bank had been closed yesterday, January 2, but Meredith had phoned first thing this morning and gotten a one o'clock appointment. She wasn't sure she could have handled it if she'd had to wait another day. Ever since she'd talked with Ava, she'd alternated between certainty that the bank would loan her the money and fear that it wouldn't. Yesterday, she'd been so nervous that her stomach had been upset.

There was no way to afford the old farmhouse without a loan, but surely, surely, the bank would come through.

And meeting with Ellen was an unexpected blessing. Meredith's appointment had been with a guy named Gary, but he had gone home sick over lunch. Unfortunate for him, but fortunate for Meredith because she and Ellen went way back. Meredith had even babysat Ellen's daughters every weekday the summer she was fifteen, when Ellen first returned to work. A conversation with her would be much easier than talking to a stranger, even if Ellen did look a lot more polished now in her plum suit and green glasses than she had when she'd started as a teller.

"Meredith, how nice to see you. What can I help you with?" Ellen adjusted a small fan on the edge of her desk, positioning it to blow on both of them and clicking it up a notch so that it drowned out the voices from the lobby. "Sorry about the heat in here. The HVAC system in this building is so old we either melt or we freeze. They really need to replace it."

"Thanks for the fan." Meredith drew in a deep breath. The cool air felt good, especially as she tried to gather her thoughts. "I'd like to talk with you about a loan."

Ellen leaned forward, one elbow on the desk, her chin resting on her knuckles.

"My Uncle Harris and Aunt Ruby are retiring and moving down to Arkansas to live near their son. I want to buy the old family farmhouse and expand my business to include a gourmet, organic restaurant. I've got a business plan worked up." Meredith dug into her purse, unfolded the three sheets of paper, and slid them across the desk.

Ellen sat back, resettled her glasses on her nose, and peered down at the first page.

"Ava worked in a restaurant in Kansas City for four years, and she finishes culinary school in June. She'd be the chef, creating a menu of farm-to-table, locally sourced food. She thinks we can easily attract diners from Columbia, sometimes even from Kansas City, who want a special destination for events like wedding anniversaries or engagements."

"Um-hum." Ellen's eyes narrowed, and she turned to the second page.

Meredith scooted back in her seat. She needed to be patient, stop interrupting, and let Ellen read. And not think about how nervous she was, or about the irony of someone like her, who almost never dated, opening a restaurant that would become a romantic destination. She bit her lip and glanced around the office.

A bowl of Dove Promises candy sat on the outside corner of Ellen's desk, asking for visitors to help themselves.

Meredith unwrapped a dark-chocolate piece and popped it in her mouth. Wasn't that just like Ellen? Considerate, offering chocolate to people who might be nervous. All Meredith's worry had been silly. She should have had more faith. Any minute now Ellen would approve the loan and then Meredith could call Ava and tell her the good news. The first step toward making her sister's dream a reality, toward paying at least part of her debt to Ava.

"Let me check a few things." Ellen pulled a calculator from the desk and tapped quickly, dark-mauve nails shining. "Well..." She frowned and clicked her fingers over the calculator again.

The tightness returned to Meredith's stomach, and all of a sudden she wished she'd prepared more for this meeting. Wished she'd painted her short, stubby nails. And wished she'd put her proposal in a binder.

But her math was solid, and though she might not appear as polished as Ellen, she ran a greenhouse, not a bank. And Ellen wouldn't care about silly things like a binder.

"Do you have any other collateral?"

"Collateral?" Meredith picked at a hangnail. She realized what she was doing and slid her hands under her thighs, trapping them between her black dress pants and the scratchy upholstery of the chair. "Well, the house and the land that Mom and Dad left Ava and me. The greenhouses. The commercial van I use for the business. And, um, my truck."

"Investments? More savings somewhere?"

"No. Just the account here at the bank." Which she'd been adding to bit by bit, even with the expense of Ava's schooling.

After her parents died, there had been a life insurance policy, but Aunt Ruby, who never had a chance to go to college, insisted that Meredith finish her degree. The money from the policy had gone to pay for her classes at community college and for living expenses for her and Ava until she finished school. If only she'd saved that money instead.

She leaned forward. "Did you see that part on page three about how I don't want to buy the whole property that's for sale, only the house and three acres?"

"I did." Ellen's eyebrows gathered in. "I'm sorry, Meredith, but we won't be able to help you. Your numbers are fine, as long as everything works out perfectly, but a good business plan needs some cushion, some provision for when things don't go well." She ran a hand over the pages Meredith had worked so hard on. "There's not any cushion here. I'm sure you know that sometimes there's a bad year."

Meredith's stomach clenched. "I grow my plants in greenhouses. It's not like I'm raising wheat or corn."

"Even so, things can happen."

"Maybe I should talk to another bank?"

"Really, I'd help you if I could. I'm pretty sure that any other bank will say the same thing. You're stretching things too thin." Ellen slid the papers back across the desk and shook her head slowly. "I'm very sorry."

An ache grew in the back of Meredith's throat. She picked up her coat, stood, and slipped it on. "Thanks for meeting with me, Ellen."

Ellen walked around the desk. "Hey, I don't say this to everyone, but you know how the way others treat you doesn't change the value God gave you? It's the same with the bank. Whether or not you can get a loan doesn't determine the value of your idea." She put a hand on Meredith's arm. "Don't give up."

Meredith gave a tense nod, then hurried through the lobby and down the block to where she'd parked her truck. Once inside, she cranked up the heat and sank into the seat, pressing her back teeth tightly together and drawing in an unsteady breath. She was not going to cry.

"Don't give up" sounded nice, but it didn't change the fact that she had no way to get a loan, no way to buy the old farmhouse, no way to make Ava's dream come true.

⤳⤳⤳

Zach pulled his SUV into the garage and shut off the air

conditioning. Normally, the weather in January in Phoenix was perfect. Today, January 3, had been downright hot.

And long. Finally, though, the end of the day had arrived. He'd tried to keep up with work during the trip to Missouri, but he'd started this morning feeling at least a month behind. Hopefully tomorrow would be better, and he'd have time to brainstorm on the next venture for Sunburst Energy.

He grabbed the carryout bag from the passenger seat, went into the house, and set the food on the granite-topped island. "Hailey, I'm home. I brought your favorite dinner from that fancy Middle Eastern restaurant you like." That should brighten their Tuesday night. The girl had a real thing for lamb wrapped in grape leaves. Once she got a whiff of the rich, spicy fragrance, she'd appear in the kitchen.

Except she didn't.

She had to be home, though. Her backpack was dumped in its normal spot near the wall in the breakfast nook.

He moved to the base of the stairs. "Hailey?"

No answer, just a thump like a door slamming shut.

Zach started up the stairs. Halfway up, he heard her crying and quickened his pace. "Hailey, what's wrong?" He knocked on her door.

"Go away." Her voice was shaky.

"Hailey, don't you want to talk about it?"

"Go away," she said more loudly.

Should he do as she asked?

He let out a silent sigh and glanced at the photos on the

hallway wall. Pictures of Hailey, Jillian, and him from when Hailey was little, from before Jillian got pregnant the second time, from when they still were the perfect happy family. *Why did you have to die, Jillian? Why couldn't you be here to help me figure out what to do?*

In September, he'd researched teenage depression online. The articles he'd found terrified him. In October, he managed to get Hailey in to see a private counselor, but after one visit, Hailey refused to go back. He'd prayed about it, but no miracles had occurred at Desert View Middle School.

Over the weekend, when he was in Missouri, he'd talked to his sister Stacey. "Treat her like you treated Jillian," she'd suggested. "At least that way she won't say you're treating her like a baby and push you away."

Okay, he'd try Stacey's advice. It definitely meant that leaving Hailey crying in her room wasn't the answer. That would have made Jillian mad. And walking in was treating Hailey like a little kid.

"I'm not going away until I'm sure you're okay," he said through the door. "You don't want me to stand here, starving to death, with a huge bag of food from Restaurant Istanbul downstairs, do you? I even got that baklava you like."

Silence, then Hailey blew her nose. "Fine. Come in."

Progress. At least a little. He opened the door.

Hailey hunkered over her bed, back against the headboard, with a pillow bunched up against her chest.

"What's going on, honey?" He sat on the foot of the bed, giving her space.

"Serena." Hailey's blue eyes grew tearier.

27

Uh-oh. Serena, star of the seventh-grade volleyball team, was the worst. There were sociopaths who were kinder. From what he'd pieced together, Serena was vicious to every kid except a select few, but polite and charming to every adult. The kind of kid who never got in trouble, no matter what they did wrong. From what he heard, about ninety percent of the time she did things he'd consider wrong.

He leaned toward Hailey. "What happened?"

She pulled the pillow up higher, hiding most of her face.

"Really, honey, you should talk. It might make you feel better, and maybe I can help."

She peeked out at him. "Right." Her tone was one-hundred percent sarcasm. "Like you helped back in September when you talked to the school counselor."

He'd thought that was a good idea.

According to Hailey, it only made things worse.

What else could he do? He couldn't call Serena's parents and tell them that their daughter should be grounded for life. He couldn't stop by the school and give Serena a piece of his mind. And he had a pretty good idea that teaching Hailey to punch Serena in the jaw wasn't the answer. "Maybe things will be better at school tomorrow."

"I have the flu."

Except for the tears and the redness her face always got when she cried, she seemed perfectly fine. No cough. No sneezing. "You don't have the flu."

"Well, I'm not going. I hate it there. All that matters to anyone is how popular you are and how much money your family has."

"We have money. We live in one of the nicest areas of Phoenix."

"Which is the only reason I don't have to sit at the loser table at lunch." She clenched the pillow tighter against her chest.

"Hailey, that can't be true. You've got friends. Like Ally. She's a nice kid."

Most of the kids at Hailey's school probably were as shallow as she said. Their parents certainly were. But Ally was different. Her mom was a kindergarten teacher. Her dad worked for the state. They were decent people, people he enjoyed talking with. In fact, Ally seemed a lot like the girls he remembered from when he was in seventh grade. A sleepover with her would solve all of Hailey's problems. "Why don't you call Ally and ask her to spend the night on Friday?"

"Al—ly." Hailey drew the word out into a lament. "Ally is going with Brock. She won't even look at me in the hall, much less talk to me." She rolled to her stomach and began to cry again.

"Oh." Zach's shoulders sank and an ache burned in his chest. What should he do now? He ran a hand over Hailey's back, but she scooted away.

For a long moment he sat there, trying to think of what to say. Every idea that came to him sounded stupid. His precious Hailey was hurting and, except for carryout Middle Eastern food, he had nothing to offer her.

Should he encourage her to eat? At least then he'd be doing something. "I'm going downstairs. I'll be there any time you want to talk or want a hug. And I'll get dinner on the table. I hope you'll come down." He gave her back a soft pat.

She rolled to the far side of the bed.

Feeling as if his lungs had been replaced with lead, he walked out of the room and left the door open. He hated this helplessness. Absolutely hated it. He liked solving problems and solving them fast. But he had no solution for this. He couldn't protect his daughter from Serena any more than he'd been able to protect Jillian from her heart condition.

Downstairs, he unpackaged the food. The dinner now seemed pretentious and overpriced. Lamb wrapped in grape leaves wasn't his favorite, and it wouldn't fix Hailey's problems. He'd rather be eating burnt ends from Whole Hog Barbecue, back in Abundance.

If only Stacey lived closer. He hadn't been able to get Hailey to talk to her much over Christmas, but if they spent more time together, he knew his sister could help. She'd been popular in high school. She'd know exactly how to handle Serena.

Stacey, though, was never moving out of Abundance.

He paused, halfway through spooning the hummus into a bowl.

His sister might not move.

But he could.

As long as he got his partner and his investors on board, he could start his next venture anywhere he wanted.

Even in his hometown of Abundance.

Chapter Three

Meredith covered the freshly sown flats with clear plastic domes to help the seeds germinate. She inhaled deeply, savoring the earthy scent of the greenhouse. She'd read that breathing in healthy bacteria from the soil affected a person's brain, making them happier, and she believed it.

But the magic of the greenhouse was more than that. It was planting tiny seeds, then watching them burst forth with life while everything outside was cold and snowy. It was, in a way, the physical embodiment of hope.

Was there any better place to work?

She strolled up and down the rows, inspecting the microgreens. First, the trays of broccoli, red cabbage, kale, and purple-stem radish she'd just planted. Then the next row, with baby plants peeping through the soil. The third row, opening their first seed leaves. The final group, which she'd planted two weeks ago, all ready to be picked, washed, and delivered tomorrow to the restaurants she supplied in Columbia. Twice a week, all year round, she seeded new flats of microgreens. Not as pretty or as interesting as the flowers that she'd plant next month to sell at the farmer's market, but steady, dependable income.

Income that would have been enough to make loan payments.

No matter how hard she tried, she hadn't been able to accept the rejection from the bank two days ago. The idea of rejoining the two pieces of property and helping Ava with her dream of running a restaurant was too good to abandon.

She'd even gone to the other bank in town yesterday, but their response had been worse than Ellen's.

"We have to follow industry standards about the amount of risk we take," the loan officer had said. "We can't hand out money to everyone who asks for it. We have a responsibility to our investors. Your idea is too much of a long shot, unless..." His face had brightened, sending a zing of hope through her, and he leaned forward as if eager to offer his suggestion. "Why don't you ask your parents if they can help you out? They might be able to co-sign."

Wow. That had stung. Of course, that loan officer was new to town. He didn't know her parents had died when she was twenty.

He didn't know that besides Ava, her only family was a great aunt she hadn't seen in a decade, Uncle Harris and Aunt Ruby, and their son, Jake.

Ava certainly didn't have any money.

Her great aunt was on a fixed income.

Cousin Jake and his wife were expecting their first child and getting their own careers started.

And Uncle Harris and Aunt Ruby were probably counting on the money from the sale of the farm to buy a place in Arkansas.

But what if they weren't? Or what if they didn't need all the money immediately? What if the idea from the guy at the bank was actually a good one?

Meredith brushed some soil off the leaves of a baby radish plant.

Wouldn't it be wonderful if it worked out?

The farmhouse would be perfect for Ava's restaurant, and, most importantly, it should stay in the family.

When Grandma and Grandpa Carlton were still alive and living there, the whole family celebrated Christmas in the farmhouse. She cherished wonderful memories of stringing popcorn and opening presents with her parents and grandparents and her aunt and uncle and cousin. Memories of being surrounded by love.

Since Grandma and Grandpa and Mom and Dad had all passed away, and if Aunt Ruby and Uncle Harris were moving, shouldn't she and Ava at least still have the house?

Really, Uncle Harris and Aunt Ruby should have offered her the chance to buy before they put it on the market.

But they probably had no idea how much restaurants paid for microgreens. Those baby plants were a lot more profitable than the zinnias and marigolds she sold at the farmer's market every spring.

Meredith smiled down at her crop, then walked out of the greenhouse and looked next door.

Uncle Harris was pulling his truck out of the garage, most likely headed to have coffee at Cassidy's Diner. With him gone, it was the perfect time to broach the subject with Aunt Ruby.

A few minutes later, Meredith peeked through Ruby's back door and spotted her at the sink, doing dishes.

Meredith cracked the door open. "Knock, kno-ock."

Ruby turned, waved her in, and dried her hands on a dish towel as she came to meet her. "Meredith, how nice to see you. Have you had breakfast? I've got homemade cinnamon raisin biscuits."

Meredith gave her aunt a quick hug. "I did have breakfast, but I'll never say no to one of your biscuits." Even though they weren't on the table, their sweet scent hovered in the room, making her mouth water.

Ruby pulled a plastic container from the refrigerator. She popped two large biscuits in the microwave, then got out the butter, poured a cup of coffee, and motioned for Meredith to join her at the table.

After Meredith had split open her biscuits and slathered them with butter, she looked over at her aunt.

Dear Aunt Ruby. At sixty-three, her short hair was more gray than brown. Her face was lined, her cheeks red from too much time in the sun and wind, and she'd put on more weight in the past few years. But her brown eyes shone with kindness. Of all the people Meredith knew, Ruby was the one who most closely lived out what the pastor said about showing God's love.

Ruby wasn't her blood relative. Uncle Harris was. He was her mom's brother. But Ruby had been the one Meredith leaned on after her parents died, the one who offered to let Ava move in so that Meredith could return to college in the fall.

In the end, though, she and Ava had wanted to be together, and it seemed best to stay in their own home. At twenty, Meredith was capable of keeping an eye on her little sister while Ava finished high school. So Meredith had transferred from the university to the community college over in Moberly, where she could commute.

All the while, though, Ruby had been next door, offering comfort and stability.

Only now she was leaving.

Meredith wiped a smear of butter off her fingers with a napkin. "I can't believe you're moving to Arkansas later this spring. I'm going to miss you so much." Just thinking about it made a lump grow in the back of her throat. She took a drink of coffee, trying to wash the emotion down.

"Oh, honey, I'm going to miss you too." Ruby reached across the table and took Meredith's hand. "You're as dear to me as my own child." Her eyes shone, and she glanced away.

Meredith held her aunt's fingers, soaking up the connection. Truly, if it hadn't been for Ruby's love, she might not have made it after Mom and Dad died. And if it hadn't been for Ruby's example, she might not have considered taking over her parents' greenhouse business as a woman alone. But Ruby made it seem, if not easy, certainly possible. How many times had she stepped in when Harris was unable to work because of his bad back? How many times had she handled the day's farm chores, and then put a delicious meal on the table, feeding not only her husband and son, but inviting Meredith and Ava over as well?

Ruby gave Meredith's fingers a quick squeeze, then sat

back with her hands in her lap. "So, what's on your mind this fine morning? I can tell you're mulling something over."

Meredith drew in a deep breath. Now or never. "You and Uncle Harris have done so much for Ava and me that I'm almost embarrassed to ask more, but..."

"Nonsense. You know I'd do anything for you, dear."

Ruby would. As for Harris? Meredith wasn't sure. He was no longer as cold to her as he had been after the accident, but he still wasn't exactly warm.

But she had to try, and asking Ruby was the place to start. "I'd like to buy your farmhouse. Not the whole farm or anything, just the house and the three acres you mow as yard." She gestured awkwardly to the window. "The bank won't loan me the money, and I was wondering if you and Harris would consider carrying the loan and letting me pay you back monthly."

Ruby's shoulders stiffened, and she ran a hand over her chin.

Except for the tick of the antique clock on the wall, the one Grandpa Carlton had bought as a wedding present for his bride, the room was silent.

"I promise I'd never miss a payment," Meredith said quickly. "Ava and I have a wonderful plan. After she graduates, we'd put a commercial kitchen in here, and she'd open a restaurant serving all organic food. I'd grow the produce right next door. We think the foodie crowd from Columbia would come, and that we could make it a real destination restaurant. Your house has so much character. It would be the perfect setting."

Ruby's face tightened. "Oh, Meredith, it's a lovely

idea. I bet it would be a huge success, but your uncle—"

"Wouldn't it be good to keep the land in the family?"

"I don't—"

"This place has been owned by Jesse Carlton or one of his descendants for four generations, and Jake's not interested in farming."

"No, Meredith, that's not it. Harris—"

"I knew it." Meredith blew out a breath. "He still blames me for Mom and Dad's death. I understand that he wants to blame someone, but surely, after all this time—"

"Meredith, stop," Aunt Ruby said loudly.

Meredith pulled back in her chair, her body rigid against the wooden frame. Aunt Ruby never raised her voice. From her, the tone was almost a physical blow.

Meredith never should have mentioned the accident, never should have said anything negative about Uncle Harris out loud. It wasn't Ruby's fault her husband was so unforgiving.

"Harris found a buyer. The deal's already done." Ruby looked away, then turned back to Meredith, eyes filled with pain. "And, oh, I've been dreading telling you this, but I can't put it off any longer. You know how Jake's wife works in real estate?"

Meredith's throat went rigid, and she nodded stiffly.

"She found a new place for us real quick. A deal we can't pass up. I'm sorry, dear, but we'll be gone by Valentine's Day."

Chapter Four

Never one to waste time implementing a plan, Zach managed the move from Arizona to Abundance in less than two months.

Once he checked the price of land in Abundance and talked with his dad and sister about what the Abundance schools were like these days, he'd known the idea was a good one.

He and his partner, Cliff, had another project in Missouri, a large solar farm near Hannibal, so they already had a good working relationship with the utility company. Zach learned of a new data center going in near Kansas City that wanted to run on all renewable energy. The business was eager to buy power produced at a solar farm outside Abundance. Cliff was supportive and more than happy to handle things in Arizona, allowing Zach to expand their business in Missouri. Plus, all their investors were fully on board.

Zach had quickly found a property that met his needs. Having a sister who was a real estate agent made it easy. Half an hour ago, just after 3 p.m. on February 20, he'd sat in the Abundance Title Company with Stacey and the agent for the sellers to sign the papers and receive the keys.

Tomorrow, Hailey would start at Abundance Middle School. Already she seemed happier than she had back in Phoenix. Why, at this very minute she was over at Dad's, playing with Stacey's four-year-old son, a little rascal who'd make anybody laugh. Kayla, the girl with the horse, had even texted saying she couldn't wait to get together.

Zach flipped his blinker and turned onto County Road 1400. He'd go back over to Dad's in time for dinner, but first he wanted to walk through the new house.

All those years, he'd stayed in Phoenix to help his daughter maintain her memories of her mom. At first, he'd thought she was so young that it wouldn't matter, but his in-laws had insisted that it was important for Hailey to grow up in the house where she could remember Jillian.

Sometimes, living in that house had brought him comfort. Other times, moving might have been easier. At every turn, the house reminded him of Jillian, of his fear throughout that second pregnancy, of his pain when both she and the baby died.

That pain…

It felt as though it might pull him under. But somehow he managed to stay strong.

For Hailey.

The first year after Jillian's death, when Hailey was seven, had been especially ugly. An endless stream of sleepless nights and exhausted days. Trying to be both mother and father to his girl. Barely pulling his weight at the office. Weaving his way in and out and back again through grief, with long periods of anger at God.

Eventually, he and Hailey got into a routine. The unthinkable life with only the two of them became normal. And he came to accept that Jillian's death hadn't been God's fault. It had been his.

Perhaps that was why he'd complied with his in-laws' wishes for so long.

Anyway, they hadn't been pleased, two weeks ago, when he told them he and Hailey were moving to Missouri. They understood, though, when he explained about how unhappy she'd been. Thank goodness, because they wouldn't have been able to change his mind. He wasn't failing his daughter in the same way he'd failed his wife.

Some people might say he overreacted in moving his business simply because his daughter was miserable. But nothing mattered more than Hailey. If she was happier in Abundance, if she was safer in a place with less crime, and if he had the flexibility, what was wrong with moving back to his hometown?

Abundance offered friends, family, small-town stability, and good values. Precisely what she needed.

All things he enjoyed as well. The town that had seemed boring and stifling after high school now felt comfortable. Familiar. Almost like a balm to his soul.

With a satisfied smile, he pulled into the drive of his new house.

But as he climbed out of his SUV, his smile faded.

The old farmhouse looked bleak and desolate. The

yard was brown, the trees bare, and over along the side of the yard, a flowerbed edged in railroad ties sat empty with nothing visible except soggy mulch. And the air was a nippy forty degrees with enough moisture in it to make it feel colder. Back in Arizona, according to Cliff, it was sunny today with an expected high of 72 degrees. Zach squeezed the keys to his new home, hoping he hadn't made a mistake.

In the distance, though, his new next-door neighbor came from around the back of her house with her dog.

That was one bright spot in the scenery, at least. "Meredith," he shouted.

Her head tilted to one side, and she gave a tentative wave.

"It's me, Zach Gilcroft," he called.

They walked toward each other, and her dog—Duke, perhaps?—galloped in a circle around them, barking the whole time.

"Hey, big fella." Zach stopped near a trio of red cedar trees at the property line, took off his gloves, and held out a hand to the dog.

The dog sniffed his fingers, apparently remembered him, and allowed Zach to scratch behind his ears as Meredith drew nearer.

Jillian wouldn't have been caught dead in jeans, muddy boots, and a brown Carhartt jacket, but somehow it looked good on Meredith. Even her navy hat, which looked as if it might have been someone's first craft project, was cute. Her dark hair shone, her cheeks were pink in the crisp winter air, and her eyes were a soft, chocolate brown.

Of course, with the way he'd ignored Meredith after

they sat together at that bonfire and then not even recognized her that day he'd run into her snowman, she wasn't going to be interested in him. And he was the last guy in the world who should be noticing how attractive a woman was. He needed to focus on the fact that Meredith would be his and Hailey's closest neighbor, something that had been one more selling point for the property. She'd handled the situation with the snowman kindly, easing Hailey's anxiety. She had a sense of humor. And, though it sounded like a bit of a pun to say it about a farmer, she was down-to-earth. All good qualities in a neighbor.

He gave Duke one last pat, and the dog wandered off.

Meredith stopped a couple of feet away, and her eyebrows quirked up. "Wow, Zach, I thought you went back in Phoenix. What are you doing here?"

"I bought the old Carlton place!" He gestured behind him. "I'm staying with Dad tonight, but tomorrow Hailey and I move in."

Her posture tensed. "Really?"

Her voice didn't hold the excitement he'd hoped for. To be honest, it didn't even hold a polite welcome. Was she still mad that he hadn't called all those years ago? They *had* gotten along great that evening. But she didn't seem mad that day in her yard last month.

"That's great." She edged backward.

What was going on? Had she found serious ruts in her lawn after the snow melted? "That offer for sod still stands, if you want it."

"My yard is fine." She glanced down, scraped mud off the toe of one boot with the other, then looked back up at him. "It's just... I didn't know who bought my aunt and uncle's place. I was sort of hoping the deal would fall through and I'd still have a chance to buy the land myself. It used to belong to my grandparents."

"Oh." The house he bought had once been her grandparents'? Wouldn't her uncle have talked with her before he listed it? Before he accepted someone else's offer?

How was Zach supposed to know that the Carltons were her grandparents? Granted, he understood way more about who was related to whom in Abundance than he ever had in Phoenix, but Meredith hadn't been in his grade at school. He didn't really know her that well, and he'd never considered who she was related to.

None of that changed the fact that he'd gotten himself in the middle of a family mess and basically bought the property out from under her.

No wonder she didn't seem thrilled to have him as a neighbor.

This was not how the move to Abundance was supposed to start.

Meredith shoved her hands in her coat pockets. Could she be any ruder?

Zach looked like a kid who had just been told he couldn't keep a stray puppy.

Aunt Ruby would be mortified by how she was acting. Meredith even heard Mom in the back of her mind, saying that she'd raised her better than this.

"I'm sorry," she said. "I can't afford the property, even if the deal had fallen through. Really, I'm glad you're moving in." After all, somebody had to live there. Why not Zach? "And I'll enjoy getting to know Hailey better."

Zach took a step closer. "The paperwork was just signed. I might be able to get things reversed. I could always buy somewhere else."

"No, no." Meredith held up a hand. "My uncle would kill me if I messed up his deal."

"Are you sure?"

"I'm sure. Honestly, I don't have the money." Nothing like dwelling on the difference in their financial positions to make the situation even more awkward. "After I heard the place sold, I've been contemplating another direction anyway."

It was true. Ever since Aunt Ruby and Uncle Harris left the day before Valentine's Day—after she'd finally stopped crying when they drove away—she'd been talking with Ava about a new plan. First, she'd get repairs done to the second greenhouse, which had been out of commission since that big wind storm a few years ago. She'd hire help and increase production. Then, once she had more income to show the bank, she'd take out a smaller loan, do some major remodeling at her house, and let Ava run the restaurant there. Meredith wasn't thrilled with the idea of having a restaurant in her home, and her house didn't have the same charm as the old farmhouse, but there was no reason they couldn't build an addition on the west side of the house, the side closer to the old farmhouse and away from the greenhouses. The greenhouses weren't particularly attractive from the outside, but they could be hidden by some well-placed latticework covered in healthy vines. Diners would have a restful view of whatever crops her new neighbor planned to raise.

And now that she thought about having Zach for a

neighbor, she rather liked the idea.

He slid his hands in his pockets. "Okay, if you're sure you don't want me to try to get the deal called off."

"I'm sure."

The lines eased on his face. "Good. I checked out a lot of properties, and this one is by far the best for my plans. Wide open space, and close to the existing power lines."

She peered over at the power line that ran to his house "Why do power lines matter?"

"Not that one. That's a distribution line that brings electricity to the house. I mean the big transmission line that goes by the southeast corner of the property."

She nodded slowly. She knew the line he meant, but she still didn't get it. "Why do you need a transmission line?"

"Remember how I told you I work in the energy sector?"

Her stomach tightened. She had a feeling she wasn't going to like this. "Yeah."

"I'm putting in a huge solar farm. You've seen solar panels on someone's roof, right?"

"I have."

"Picture fifty acres of those in rows on the ground, all angled to face south."

She stared out at the field where Uncle Harris had grown soybeans.

"I'll leave some yard around the house for Hailey and me, and I'll lease out most of the land on the other side of the house to be planted in traditional crops, but the fifty acres closest to you, between the back yard and that transmission line, is going to be covered in solar panels."

The cold February air suddenly made her cough. She held up a finger to indicate that she'd be able to talk in a minute, looked past Zach at the fields behind his house, and then back at him. "Really? Solar panels?"

"On a good day, we'll create enough power for all of Springfield. That transmission line will carry the energy we produce to our customer in Kansas City. There's not as much sunlight here as in Arizona, but certainly enough to make a healthy profit." He glanced over his shoulder, as if envisioning rows of equipment, then turned back to her. "And it will let me move back home. Hailey needs to be around more family and more kids with better values."

"I see." Meredith swallowed.

What she saw was that, although in theory she was a big fan of renewable energy, she didn't like this particular project.

With effort she managed to keep her tone light. "That sounds like a good plan. Really good. I respect you for making changes to help your daughter. She seemed like a sweet girl." Meredith took a half-step back toward her house. "And welcome to the neighborhood. Duke and I have to go, but I'm sure I'll be seeing you." She waved and started home.

Home, where she and Ava would never open their restaurant, no matter how much remodeling she did.

No one in Columbia was going to drive all the way to Abundance to eat an all-organic gourmet meal in a restaurant with a scenic view of solar panels. There wasn't enough latticework in all the world.

What was she going to do now?

Chapter Five

Zach propped a board on Meredith's porch. "An offering."

"What's this?" Meredith's forehead scrunched up. She stepped out her front door, zipped up her gray hoodie, and peered at the plank.

Hopefully she wouldn't think it was silly. When he'd come up with the idea last night, it had seemed like a good way to smooth things over. He didn't want bad relations with a neighbor before he'd even finished unpacking. Especially not Meredith. He pointed to the plank. "It's from the farmhouse. I had someone come over yesterday and start redoing the half bath on the first floor."

Meredith raised her eyebrows. "Ooh, you mean you don't love the way all that green tile from the 1970s makes the room feel as if it's closing in on you?"

"You've felt it too?"

"My sister and I always referred to that bathroom as 'the pit,' because it's like being trapped inside an avocado."

"A perfect description. Plus, it's got that very attractive harvest gold sink and toilet." He chuckled. "Anyway, a woman I know from high school who does remodeling was available, so I booked her. She's supposed to be excellent." Possibly not the smartest plan, since the farmhouse was already in chaos with boxes left to unload, but Zach did like the idea of moving forward. "She took out some drywall late yesterday and found this behind it." He turned the plank around, revealing the side that was painted white. "Check it out."

Meredith leaned closer and peered at the handwriting on the board, her dark hair blowing in the crisp morning breeze.

"Oh, my goodness!" She pointed to a line and a date on the board. "That's my grandpa's name. It says he was five foot two. From the date, he must have been about ten." She ran a finger down the names and dates. "This is Great-Uncle Timothy, and here's Great-Aunt Bess. They've all passed away, but…wow."

"The handwriting looks like a woman's. So maybe your great-grandmother was the one to measure her kids' heights against the wall?"

"I bet she was. Nora Spotts Carlton. How cool is that?" Meredith's eyes sparkled.

He held the plank toward her. "Would you like it? Since you weren't able to buy the family farmhouse, it might be one way to hold on to your family history." And possibly improve things between the two of them.

"I'd love it. Thank you."

"You're welcome."

She took the board and rested it, upright, against the

side of her house, then turned back to face him. "I have to admit, though, it wasn't only emotion that made me want to buy the farmhouse. It was also business."

"Oh? You wanted to expand your greenhouses?" From what he'd seen out his bedroom window, she had two greenhouses, but one of them was out of service. Besides, from researching his own property, he knew she had five acres. Plenty of room to put in a third or even a fourth greenhouse if she wanted. She didn't need his property to expand.

"My sister is finishing culinary school, and we planned to open a restaurant in the old farmhouse. I'd grow the organic vegetables, and she'd run the restaurant. This place"—she gestured behind her—"that my parents built before I was born doesn't have the character or the space."

The tidy blue ranch house was attractive, but nothing out of the ordinary. "Maybe with the right renovations…"

"Yeah, I considered that for a while." She looked down. "But I'm not sure an organic restaurant with a view of solar panels is going to have the rustic, restful vibe we were aiming for."

His chest deflated. "Oh, man. I'm sorry." It didn't matter how thoughtful he'd been with the plank and the record of her family's heights. He'd not only bought her heritage out from under her, he'd totally destroyed her business plan.

"Don't worry about it." She raised her chin. "I'll come up with another idea. There has to be a way."

"That's the spirit." If only every small business owner had her tenacity. He'd mentored a few who…

Hold on.

"Hey, I've coached a lot of start-ups. You wouldn't want to have dinner with me and talk about your business, would you? I might have some ideas that would help."

She stood up taller. "Really? You'd do that?"

"I'd be happy to. Consider it my way of making up for the fact that I bought the property you wanted." He ran through his calendar in his mind. His week was jam-packed, but he hated to put Meredith off.

Last night, though, Hailey had asked if she could spend the night with Kayla on Friday. He was pretty sure the girls would spend the whole time planning how to convince him to buy Hailey a horse, but it did give him a free evening. "What about Whole Hog Barbecue on Friday at six?"

"That sounds wonderful," Meredith said quickly.

"Excellent. Since we live right next door, shall I pick you up and we ride together?"

"Okay. I'll be ready." She picked up the plank. "Thanks for this. It was really nice of you."

He grinned, waved, and started down her porch stairs.

In spite of their rough start as neighbors, one day she might say that having him move in next door had been the best thing that ever happened to her business.

The following morning, Meredith went outside to get a log for the fire from the pile at the side of the house. The last week of February and it was still as cold as early January.

Across the road, Hailey leaned against the same fence post where Meredith and Ava and cousin Jake had waited for the school bus. Her turquoise coat was zipped all the way up, her shoulders hunched, and her arms crossed over her chest as if she might be wishing she was back in Arizona.

This spring had not been very welcoming.

But Meredith could be. She waved and gave Hailey a big smile.

Hailey waved back, and then disappeared as the bus drove up.

Meredith went inside, added the log to the fire, and gave the embers a good stir. Then she stood at the window in her kitchen, looking at her aunt and uncle's—at Zach and Hailey's house.

Hailey seemed like such a sweet girl.

And even if Zach had bought the old farmhouse, even if his plans for a solar farm meant she and Ava couldn't expand this house and use it for a restaurant, he was willing to give her business advice.

That was a good thing.

But she had to remember the purpose of dinner tomorrow night—business.

No matter what she wanted to read into the situation, she wasn't repeating past mistakes.

Even now, sixteen years later, she remembered the time she and Zach had sat together at a bonfire the summer after she'd graduated from high school. The hours they'd spent, staring into the fire and talking. The way he'd put his arm around her when the temperature dropped, pulling her close beside him on the hay bale. The tight squeeze he'd given her hands when they said goodnight at her car.

He hadn't kissed her, but he'd had a husky note in his voice that had made her sure he'd call the next day. Mom had even teased her about hovering by her phone.

Only he didn't call.

Not the next day or the next week or…ever.

Back then, she never should have gotten her hopes up. Zach had been a year older, already through his freshman year of college, and far too popular to date a girl like her. A couple of weeks later, she heard he'd started seeing a girl his age who'd been a cheerleader at Abundance High.

So today she needed to keep his invitation to dinner—wait, correct that, his invitation *to discuss her greenhouses*—in perspective.

She needed to focus on business.

Like the fact that whatever she and Ava decided on, they needed more capital.

The best way to get that was to do more with what she had.

Not only scrimping and saving and making every dollar count, but also using the resources of her greenhouse business in a way that would make them grow, just like her plants. If she looked at things from that light, even if they needed a different location for the restaurant, getting the second greenhouse up and running still seemed like a good idea.

She probably should have gotten it repaired a long time ago. But it was damaged right about the time her assistant got so unreliable that Meredith let her go. A few days later, one of the restaurants she supplied went out of business. At that point, the repairs hadn't seemed worth the expense. She scaled back, did all the work herself, and didn't need the extra space.

But now it seemed like a missed opportunity.

She got out a pencil and a legal pad, sat at the kitchen table, and made some notes. Eventually she checked the time to make sure Ava wasn't in class, set her phone on the table, put it on speaker, and dialed. "I've got an idea about the restaurant," she announced.

"You're going to lobby the county commissioners to get them to stop Zach from putting in all those solar panels?"

"That would never work. Pretty much, you can do whatever you want with your own land out here in the county."

"Yeah. You're right. So, what's your idea?"

"Well, I was thinking about Zach and how we're getting together to talk more about my greenhouse business, and I realized that smart business people do more with what they already have. I need to get the second greenhouse up and running. If I hire someone to help me..." Meredith made a note on her pad to start asking around.

"You've had a hard time in the past finding someone you could count on."

"Yeah. It has to be the right person, someone who's meticulous and conscientious. But if I find that person and expand my production of microgreens, possibly add some heirloom tomatoes and herbs, I can save money faster. We can buy a building somewhere else, like in town by the antique shop on Main Street. A restaurant featuring locally sourced produce from a few miles away still sounds like something we could advertise."

"Getting the second greenhouse running again sounds smart," Ava said. "And it does seem like we need more assets."

"It might take a year or two to save up enough to satisfy the bank."

"After I graduate, I can get a job in Kansas City and save for the restaurant too. I bet I could get hired again at The Table. But"—Ava's words slowed— "what's this about you talking more with Zach Gilcroft?"

Meredith tucked her thumbs under the outside of her thighs and clutched the edges of the seat of the wooden kitchen chair. Woops. She shouldn't have mentioned her plans with Zach. She could only imagine where Ava's mind had gone. "We're getting together for dinner tomorrow night. He's going to help me with my business plan."

Ava cleared her throat dramatically. "Tomorrow night?"

"Yeah." Meredith had been surprised herself when he suggested a Friday night. They could just as easily discuss the greenhouse business over coffee one morning in her kitchen.

"Is he picking you up?"

"It makes sense to ride together. We live right next door."

"Mer-e-di-th." Ava drew the word out into four syllables. "If a guy picks you up and takes you out to dinner on Friday night, it's a date."

"Nope. Not always." Despite the fact that Ava couldn't see her, Meredith shook her head resolutely. She wasn't letting her hopes go skipping down that path, and she wasn't going to allow Ava to fill her head with romantic fantasies.

"I can't believe it." Ava's words rang with delight. "You're going out on a date with Zach Gilcroft, the guy you mooned over for an entire summer."

"It is *not* a date. And I did not moon over him for an entire summer."

"Oh, yes, you did. Don't you remember all the times we went to the pizza place because he had a summer job there?"

She'd forgotten that. And wished Ava had forgotten it as well. It made her sound as if she'd had a major crush on the guy and…okay, maybe she had. For a week or two.

"Now he lives next door, and he's taking you out! Where are you going? What are you wearing?"

"Ava." Meredith slid into her firmest I'm-the-adult-in-charge voice, the one she'd used when her sister was in high school and decided she wouldn't do chores around the house. "You are blowing this way out of proportion."

"I'm not. I don't care if you don't officially call it a date." Ava sniffed. "Your official dates happen what? Once a year?"

Meredith crossed her arms and scowled at the phone. So what if she didn't date much? She had her reasons, even if she didn't want to discuss them with Ava. "It's not like I have a lot of free time, running this business by myself. The watering alone—"

"I know, I know. But still…"

"Plus, most men my age in Abundance are already married with three kids."

"Which is precisely why you need to change your mindset about dinner with Zach tomorrow night."

Meredith rubbed her temples. "Ava, let's get back to the greenhouse operation. The dinner is no big deal. It's not like we're going to some candlelit hideaway. We're getting barbecue at Whole Hog."

"Aw, you're no fun." Ava gave an audible sigh. "But fixing the second greenhouse does make sense. Before that windstorm, it was fine. I know you're really busy running things all on your own, but if you can hire someone good, at least part time, I think you can make this work."

"Me too. I'll try to get a repair guy out here to give me an estimate. And I'll search online for restaurants in Columbia, and think about how I might one day expand my client list."

"Hey, I've got to go, but it sounds good."

Meredith hung up. The plan did sound good. She could even talk to her current clients about heirloom tomatoes and herbs, and ask if there were any other vegetables they'd like to source locally.

And today…

Well, despite what she'd said, after she called about getting the plastic repaired on the greenhouse, she might get her hair trimmed.

And buy some new mascara.

And try on an outfit or two to decide what to wear when she went out to dinner with Zach.

Chapter Six

Thursday lunch was hopping at Cassidy's Diner. His sister had run in at the last minute, so it was a good thing Zach had gotten here early and grabbed a table.

"I'll have the fried pork tenderloin sandwich with potato salad and a fruit cup." He handed the plastic-covered menu to Grace, the owner of Cassidy's Diner, and shifted his weight in the vinyl booth, searching for a comfortable spot.

"I'll have the chef salad," Stacey said. "With blue cheese dressing on the side."

Grace scribbled on her pad. "Coming right up."

Zach sat silent for a moment, taking in the buzz of conversation from the crowd of diners, the ding of the bell that the cook rang when he slid plates out from the kitchen, the smell of fried food, and the sign advertising the pies of the day: Kentucky Derby, Cherry, and Butterscotch Cream. Even when he'd lived in Phoenix, he'd eaten here every time he was back in Abundance. Cassidy's Diner had been a part of his life since before he could remember.

"Meeting here for lunch was a good idea, Stace." Zach took a drink of coffee. "Thanks for suggesting it." He was enjoying being back home even more than he'd expected. There was something nice about knowing his dad and his sister and her family were nearby. People he could count on, no matter what.

Hopefully Stacey could even tell him what was going on with Hailey's English teacher.

"I'm really glad you're back in town." Stacey's phone dinged, and she typed frantically into it, both thumbs flying.

Zach sipped his coffee and, after realizing he might be waiting a while, made a mental count of the number of people in the room he knew, the people he didn't know, and the people who he was supposed to know but couldn't remember their names.

Eventually, he'd get all the names straight again. In the meantime, one name kept popping up in his mind—Meredith. He was eager to talk more with her tomorrow night. He liked brainstorming with other entrepreneurs, and he'd been impressed by her attitude. Dinner with her would be a nice way to end the work week.

Finally, Stacey shoved her phone in her purse. "Sorry, I listed two new homes this morning, and I have to keep on top of the details."

"No problem. Two new listings today, huh? Your real estate business sounds as if it's doing great."

"It's been going well, but I tell you, between work and raising George, I am worn out." She took a long sip of her

Diet Pepsi, then clutched the clear plastic cup to her chest. "This is going to be my life blood today. I need every ounce of caffeine I can get after last night."

"What happened last night?"

Grace approached, and Stacey smiled as she served her chef salad. "Thank you. This is lovely."

Zach looked at the plate now before him. The pork was breaded and fried golden-brown, the sandwich was enormous, and it smelled incredible. He drew in a deep breath and gave Grace a big thumb's up.

Stacey dumped her dressing over her salad and scraped the last drops out of the plastic cup.

Which kind of made ordering dressing "on the side" irrelevant. Luckily, he'd learned at a young age not to point out things like that to his older sister.

She forked a bite of boiled egg. "I swear, George will be the death of me. Last night, after we finally got him in bed, we noticed that the house seemed cold. The furnace had shut off. Earl Ray tinkered around but couldn't figure it out." She dipped the bite of egg in a glob of dressing. "Since it was supposed to get down close to zero last night, we called a service—I use them a lot for work—and they came over about an hour later. The guy checked everything he could think of. Finally, at nearly midnight, he noticed that *someone* had stuck a tennis ball in the exhaust for the gas furnace."

"Someone?" Zach bit into his sandwich. It tasted even more delicious than it smelled.

"Uh-huh." Stacey ate the bite of egg and rolled her eyes. "Someone who's four years old and had already had a big day, what with tracking mud all over my kitchen floor and telling his preschool teacher that she had a nose like a pig."

"I wonder why he put a tennis ball in the exhaust pipe."

"Earl Ray asked him that this morning. George said it fit perfectly, and he thought it was a good place to store it."

Zach chewed another bite of sandwich and pictured the exhaust at the old farmhouse. A tennis ball probably did fit perfectly.

"Don't you go looking like you agree with him. His storage solution meant I didn't get to bed until one in the morning, and it cost us a fortune for an after-hours service call." She jabbed at a cherry tomato in her salad. "And the HVAC guy is going to rib me about this for months."

Zach snickered. "So, does George's preschool teacher have a nose like a pig?"

Stacey sighed. "Well, yeah. A little."

Zach laughed. "Stacey, you should have expected this when you married Earl Ray. He was always getting in trouble. Don't you remember the time in high school when he put manure in a paper grocery bag, set it right outside the principal's window, and lit it on fire so the principal would run out and stomp on it?"

"Hmph." Stacey twisted up her lips and ate another bite of her salad. "Things like that are a lot funnier when they're done by your boyfriend than when they're done by your child. When Earl Ray pulled stupid stunts, I never had to deal with the consequences."

Zach took a large bite of potato salad. Sometimes, a wise man knew it was better to eat than to speak.

Stacey blew out a long breath. "It's a good thing I love

George and Earl Ray as much as I do." Her face softened into an expression that, though Zach wouldn't say it out loud, could only be called googly-eyed. It was clear that no matter what her husband or her son did, Stacey adored them.

Zach kept eating, appreciating his lunch. He might get some pie to take home to have after dinner with Hailey. Perhaps a couple of slices of cherry.

After a moment, Stacey looked at Zach. "I haven't even asked how Hailey's doing, and that's the main reason I wanted to have lunch. Does she seem happier here than back in Phoenix?"

"She does. She's really liking that girl Kayla and some friends of hers."

"Is that Kayla Stark?"

"Uh-huh."

"Her mom's a sweetheart."

Zach stretched his elbows out to his sides, loosening the tension in his shoulders. His right elbow came near the window, near the cold seeping through the glass.

Icy windows, and that dip down to two degrees last night. Winter in Missouri was quite a change from Phoenix, but so far he'd found it refreshing. Probably next year he'd be less enthused, but right now it felt new, and new was good.

Pretty much, he liked everything about being back home, except for one thing.

"Hey." He leaned forward and lowered his voice. "What have you heard about an English teacher named Mrs. Dawson? She assigns a ton of reading, and she seems a little obsessive, insisting that the kids write a page every single day, even on the weekends and spring break, in their 'Creativity Journal.'"

Stacey swirled her drink with her straw. "One of my clients mentioned that. It probably does seem like a lot of work, starting midyear, but I hear she's a good teacher. Why don't you give it some time?"

Give it time? That's all his sister had to offer? "You don't think I should ask to have Hailey transferred to another class?"

"Of course not. Moving back here was an excellent idea, but you can't fix everything for her. Some stuff you have to let her complain about and figure out how to solve by herself."

Well, yeah, he knew that. But he didn't like the nightly crises when Hailey was already in bed and then remembered she hadn't written her page for the day.

Of course, there were other solutions. She should be writing that page with the rest of her homework, not saving it for when inspiration struck like she claimed to be doing. Creativity, or a creative solution to a problem, didn't appear out of the mist. A person had to sit down and work at it. Play with different ideas until a good one came along.

"And"—Stacey gestured to him with a forkful of lettuce—"if you spend less time thinking about Hailey's problems, you can focus more on your own life." Her eyes took on an unsettling gleam. "Like meeting someone here in Abundance. You never talk much about who you dated in Phoenix, but I've got a friend you'd get along great with."

Whoa. He held up a hand to put the brakes on that idea. "Uh, thanks, Stace, but no thanks. I'm sure if I want to date in Abundance, I can find someone myself." The last thing he needed was his sister playing matchmaker. "Anyway, I'm far too busy to see anyone right now."

"Zach, you and Destiny would make the perfect couple."

"Sis, you know what it's like starting a business. It's not a good time."

Stacey mashed the last little bits of blue cheese between her fork tines, working hard to get every single particle of cheese out of her empty salad bowl. "I guess, but you need more in your life than work."

He put the last of his sandwich in his mouth and shook his head, trying to appear regretful.

He was thirty-five years old. He was not going out with anyone shoved on him by his older sister.

Even if he found someone nice, he wasn't interested in dating. Not after what happened with Jillian.

Stacey plucked up her ticket and hitched her purse strap onto her shoulder. "I've got to run, but you think about it. I've known you since the day you were born and, in my opinion, all your fast-paced deals are simply an attempt to fill the void in your life. It's been six years. You need to find someone."

Before he could swallow and tell her she was wrong, she patted his arm and hurried toward the counter.

As he ate his last bite of fruit salad, the diner owner came out and erased cherry pie from the chalkboard.

Great. Minimal advice on Hailey. Maximum interference in his life.

And because he got caught up listening to Stacey blather about some woman named Destiny, he missed out on the kind of pie he wanted.

Maybe moving close to family wasn't as wonderful as he'd thought.

Meredith angled the hand mirror and tipped her head from side to side late Thursday afternoon, watching the reflection of the back of her hair in the bathroom mirror. It looked healthier after the trim, and the stylist had shown her a different way to curl it. With the new cut and the mascara she'd bought at the drugstore right before she came home—mascara that was guaranteed to make her lashes long, thick, and luxurious—she might not look too bad tomorrow night when she had dinner with Zach.

When she had dinner with Zach. She swirled the words in her mind, lingering on every syllable as she set the hand mirror on her bathroom counter and went to the kitchen. *She* was having dinner with Zach Gilcroft. A tingle ran through her chest just thinking about it. Oh, sure, he'd asked because he felt guilty about buying Aunt Ruby and Uncle Harris's property. Even so, it was her teenage dream come true. Okay, it was also her current-day dream come true. Despite all the lectures she'd given herself, she couldn't help but be a little excited. She pulled her arms close against her sides, hugging tight the anticipation of the evening.

The doorbell rang.

She walked into the front hall, Duke on her heels.

Hailey waved through the window.

Meredith opened the door, and Duke wriggled out. "Hi, Hailey."

"Hi." Hailey bent down and said hello to Duke,

rubbing his ears. "I hate to bug you, but is there any way you can come over for a few minutes? Dad's not home and the contractor lady ran to the hardware store and Drama Club is having a party tomorrow night and I wanted to bring cupcakes. I set the timer for the minimum baking time on the box, but how can I tell if that's long enough?"

"I'd be happy to help." Meredith waved Hailey in and slid on the boots in the drip tray. "Just give me a second to zip these."

Duke edged toward the door.

"You're staying here, boy," Meredith said. "You're not known for your baking skills."

Hailey gave him one more pat and followed Meredith outside. They strolled along the road in the late afternoon sunshine, their breath making puffy white clouds.

It was a little odd that Hailey had asked for help with her cupcakes. Meredith would have assumed that a girl her age would run an internet search for "How to Tell When Cupcakes Are Done" and find fifty-three videos with demonstrations. Maybe she was lonely, though, being in a new town with her dad not home, and the cupcakes were an excuse to talk to someone.

Once they reached the old farmhouse, Hailey opened the back door and led the way in.

Two steps into the kitchen, an ache filled Meredith's chest.

Ruby wasn't there.

Meredith thought she'd accepted the fact that her aunt and uncle had moved, but somehow she still expected to see Ruby smiling by the sink, offering her coffee, waiting to hug her. The reaction was natural, of course. For so many years, Ruby had been right next door, filling the void left when Mom and Dad died. This kitchen had been the place to go for comfort.

Now Ruby was four hundred miles away in Arkansas, eager to welcome her first grandchild into the world. Meredith had been left here to fend for herself.

Alone.

Part of that feeling came from Ava going back to school. Part of it was because Meredith worked by herself. And part of it existed because the greenhouse took long hours, hours that often meant she couldn't accept invitations to spend time with friends.

Sometimes she felt so alone it seemed even God didn't care about her. Or at least not as much as He cared about other people. That didn't really make sense, but knowing that didn't seem to change her emotions.

It hadn't always been that way. Certainly not when she was growing up.

These days... Was it because of the way Uncle Harris treated her? Was she somehow confusing his opinion with God's? Or was it her guilt? Whatever it was, she couldn't shake the feeling.

Which was probably why, even though she attended church every week as she'd been raised, she didn't think much about God the rest of the week. Or sometimes, not even during the service. These days, church was more a time to see people, listen to nice music and—during the sermon—plan the week ahead.

Anyway, whatever the reason, if Hailey was lonely, Meredith understood.

And having Ruby move away only made it worse.

Yeah, with Harris's back problems, it made sense that he and Ruby had retired. And Ruby was so excited about becoming a grandmother.

Plus, it wasn't like Meredith was a kid anymore. She was a grown woman.

Maybe it was her turn to care for someone else, her turn to give comfort.

Sure, Hailey had her dad, and Zach's sister Stacey was a real estate agent here in town, and his dad lived in Abundance too. Sometimes, though, like now, Hailey might need someone next door. Might even need someone to give her a hug after a bad day at school if her dad wasn't around. If Meredith could be that person, she would be carrying on Ruby's legacy.

So she raised her chin and walked toward the stove. "It smells incredible in here! Are the cupcakes chocolate?"

"Double fudge." Hailey pointed to the box on the kitchen table. "And I had Dad buy chocolate frosting too."

"I bet they're almost done. Where are the hot pads?"

Hailey pulled a stack of hot pads and oven mitts from a drawer.

Meredith arranged four hot pads on the kitchen table and opened the oven door. Two pans of chocolate cupcakes waited inside.

"See how they're nice and round on top, with no spots that look mushy?"

Hailey leaned in and nodded.

"That means they're probably done. Are you okay taking them out?"

"Sure." Hailey grinned. "I'm not afraid of the oven. Dad's taught me all he knows about making frozen pizza."

Meredith handed her the mitts.

Hailey removed the cupcakes from the oven and carefully set them on the table.

"My aunt always checked them like this." Meredith tapped the biggest cupcake on the peak of its rounded top. "See how it bounces back? It's done."

Hailey tapped a cupcake from the other pan.

It bounced back instantly.

"Now you just wait a few minutes and then take them out to let them cool." Meredith leaned over the pans and inhaled deeply. "And try not to eat them all before tomorrow's party."

Hailey beamed at the cupcakes like a proud mother, then looked up at Meredith. "Thank you for helping me."

"Any time. Would you like me to give you a hand with the dishes?"

"Would I?" Hailey sounded as if she'd been offered front row tickets to see the latest hit band. "That would be wonderful. Dad's so insistent that if I make a mess in the kitchen, I have to clean it up."

"That seems pretty reasonable."

"I think it's mostly because he hates doing dishes."

Meredith chuckled and picked up a dishrag. In no time at all, the two of them had the kitchen cleaned. The dishes done, the counters wiped and—since Zach didn't seem to own a cooling rack—the cupcakes lined up on waxed paper.

Now... would it be rude to ask? Even though the farmhouse wasn't hers, she was eager to see the end of the avocado bathroom.

If a building could have a sense of pride, this place had suffered for years. A house that displayed so much style—

a curved second-floor balcony, elaborate trim inside and out, and a turret—must have wished it could cry out in protest when Grandpa installed the half bath with its overabundance of avocado.

Meredith glanced toward the hall. "I should head home, but before I go, would you mind if I took a peek at the remodel? I don't mean to be nosy but—"

"Help yourself." Hailey pointed toward the half bath but let her hand drop. "I guess you know where it is, don't you? Dad told me you wanted this house, and we bought it from your relatives." Her mouth thinned and what looked like worry flashed through her eyes.

The last thing Meredith wanted to do was make the girl uncomfortable. "I do know where it is," she said gently. "And I do miss my aunt and uncle, but I'm awfully glad to have you as a new neighbor."

Hailey's chest swelled. "Thanks. I like having you as a new neighbor too."

A warm coziness filled Meredith's heart as she went into the hall. Being a good neighbor, possibly even a mentor to Hailey, felt right.

She peeked into the half bath. Every square of avocado tile had been removed. The harvest gold sink and toilet were gone. The ugly linoleum had been ripped up, leaving nothing but plywood on the floor. And the room had been enlarged, taking space from what used to be a little nook for someone to talk on the landline telephone. That was probably where the board with the height measurements had been found. "This is such an improvement already," she called out to Hailey as she stepped back in the hall.

There in the hall, on the wall across from the

bathroom, was a large, framed photo of Zach, a much younger Hailey, and a beautiful woman.

Not merely beautiful. Gorgeous. In a way that blasted the warm coziness out of Meredith's heart like a gust of wind coming through an open door in January.

"Did you see the new tile stacked up in the corner?" Hailey came down the hall. "Dad let me help pick it out."

Tile? Meredith hadn't noticed any tile. "Is this your mom?" She pointed to the photo.

"Yeah." Hailey's voice grew sad. "That was taken a few months before she died. She was pregnant, but you can't really tell."

No, she couldn't tell at all. The woman was slenderer than Meredith on her best day. "She's lovely. You look a lot like her."

"That's what Dad says. She won a bunch of beauty pageants, you know."

Meredith's stomach sank. A beauty queen. "I can see why." She wasn't sure what else to say. "I, um, need to head out." She walked back toward the kitchen.

Hailey scurried behind her. "Do you want a cupcake to take home? They aren't frosted yet but—"

"No, thanks. You save them for the Drama Club." Even unfrosted, one of those cupcakes was probably two hundred calories, the last thing Meredith needed after seeing Miss Skinny-As-a-Model-Even-While-Pregnant. She slipped on her coat, told Hailey goodbye, and headed home.

A new haircut and mascara would never make Zach Gilcroft interested in someone like her.

The man dated cheerleaders. And married a beauty queen.

There was no use getting her hopes up. No use courting disappointment.

His "date" with her tomorrow night was a chance for business advice.

Nothing more.

Chapter Seven

"There's a spot."

Zach turned his head.

Meredith pointed between two pickups in the back parking lot at Whole Hog Barbecue.

Zach squeezed his SUV between them. "I didn't expect this place to be so busy, especially since the weather might get bad later."

"If we do get ice, it's not supposed to happen until two or three hours from now." Meredith unhooked her seatbelt and opened her door. "Besides, it's Friday night, and there's not much else to do except watch the high school basketball game."

He'd been so busy dealing with permits for the new solar farm that he hadn't thought of that. And until he drove into the parking lot, he hadn't thought of what the Abundance rumor mill would churn out once he and Meredith were seen together on a Friday night, a night most people considered a date night.

Folks in Abundance didn't know that he almost never dated. In fact—he grimaced as he shut his car door—Meredith didn't know that either.

Aaargh. This evening was supposed to make things better with his new neighbor, not more awkward. The last thing he wanted was give her the impression that there was anything romantic between them.

He'd have to make sure that after some polite chitchat, the conversation would be strictly about her business plans. Friendly, but nothing more. Tomorrow, he'd call Stacey and beg her to squelch any rumors she heard.

He fell in step with Meredith as they walked toward the front of the restaurant. "Hey, you got me thinking about basketball. How's the Abundance High team this year?"

"Pretty good."

Zach nodded. He wouldn't mind going to a game, reliving his high school glory days a bit. "Is Tesson still the head coach?"

"Yep."

"He was good. Strict, but fair."

They rounded the corner of the building, and Zach opened the door and followed Meredith in. Her dark hair swung, waves rippling as she moved. He wasn't sure, but he didn't remember the curls from when he'd seen her two days ago.

Once inside, warm air surrounded them, and a waitress passed by carrying a tray filled with food.

Meredith's eyes lit up. "Just smell those onion rings!"

"I know." He caught a glimpse of a half rack of ribs before the waitress disappeared behind a group of men who were leaving. "A table for two, please," he said to the hostess.

"Five minutes," she said. "The place is hopping tonight."

It was. The whole restaurant hummed with conversation, punctuated by an occasional burst of laughter.

From a table a few feet in, a dark-haired woman waved. After a second, the man across the table from her turned and added a quick wave of his own.

Zach raised a hand in reply. "That's Becky Hamlin. We're related, sort of. She's my sister's husband's sister. That's her husband, Seth, with her."

"I know." Meredith waved at them. "Becky and I had some classes together in high school."

Zach could almost hear the rumor mill starting to turn. He'd have to ask Stacey to call Becky first thing and casually mention that he and Meredith had been having a business meeting.

The two of them moved toward the padded bench near the door, and Meredith took off her gloves and unzipped her coat.

"Here, let me." He helped her out of her coat, trying not to notice the way her bright-red sweater fell over her curves. Maybe he didn't date, but he wasn't blind. Meredith was an attractive woman. Not drop-dead gorgeous the way Jillian had been. More cute and wholesome but appealing all the same.

"I love Whole Hog." Meredith took her coat from him, sat, and folded it over her lap. "The food is delicious, and there's something so nice about being around people you know." She shrugged and spread her hands, palms up. "I guess I'm just a small-town girl at heart."

Zach sat beside her. "I know what you mean." Despite his concerns about gossip, he understood. "It was exciting living in a city with lots of things to do. For a while I thought that was what I wanted, but I missed this. I missed Cassidy's and Whole Hog. I missed my family and the sense of community."

"I have your table ready," the hostess said.

They followed her into the seating area, and with each step, the smell of slow-cooked meat, tangy sauce, onion rings, and fries grew stronger. At last the hostess stopped at a corner table, where a waitress set down water glasses. Two minutes later, she walked away with their order.

Zach moved his silverware and napkin to one side and rested his arms on the table. They'd had the right amount of polite conversation. Now it was time for business.

Meredith leaned forward. "So, why did you move away? Did you simply want to see what it was like in the big city?"

"Partly." Apparently a little more conversation was needed. He could do that. "I moved to Phoenix because my wife, Jillian, wanted to. She got a job as a buyer for a department store after we finished college." Enough about Jillian. "Speaking of college, weren't you at Truman State?"

"I started out there." Meredith's voice grew softer. "I finished up at the community college over in Moberly, because I needed to commute after the accident."

Ugh. He hadn't meant to take the conversation anywhere near her parents' deaths. Now that he had, he couldn't avoid the subject. "My dad told me about your parents being killed in a car wreck when you were in college. I'm really sorry."

"Thanks." She glanced down, sighed, and looked back up. "I'm sorry about your wife. Was it a car accident too?"

Zach's mouth went dry. "Uh, no." Now would be a great time for the waitress to bring their food, but she was nowhere to be seen. "Jillian had complications with her second pregnancy. Both she and our baby died."

Meredith's face crumpled. "Zach, I'm so sorry. I guess they can do a lot with modern medicine, but sometimes it's not enough."

He shifted in his seat. He was totally bungling this evening. First of all, he never should have suggested they meet on a Friday night. And now, instead of business, they'd somehow ended up talking about personal stuff, very personal stuff that he normally didn't discuss with anyone.

He cleared his throat and reached toward his jacket. He'd get a pen from his coat pocket, write *Business Plan* on the paper place mat, underline it, and end this impromptu therapy session.

He looked over at Meredith again.

Her eyes were shining, as if her kindness was radiating out.

His heart tightened, and an ache spread through his chest. An ache that for some stupid reason seemed as if it might be eased by talking about Jillian.

Right. Like he was ever going to do that.

But he let his coat fall back on the vinyl seat beside him, the pen still in the pocket.

Was it because he was home in Abundance? Because he and Meredith had connected at the bonfire long ago? Because enough time had passed that he was ready to talk?

Whatever the reason, he blurted out the truth. "Jillian had a heart condition. Her doctor told her after Hailey was born that she shouldn't have another child. She wanted another baby so much, though, that I went along with it. If I hadn't, she wouldn't have died." He shook his head. "She had complications at twenty weeks. There was nothing the doctors could do for her or for our son."

Meredith's eyes softened, then her face grew rigid and she leaned toward him. "Her death," she said firmly, "is not your fault."

Zach rolled his eyes. The same old story. Exactly what his pastor back in Arizona had said.

"Your wife was a grown woman. She made the decision to take the risk."

Meredith's words resonated inside him.

His pastor hadn't said that, hadn't placed any blame at all.

But it *had* been Jillian's decision, Jillian's idea, Jillian's faul—

No. Zach wouldn't go there. He could go for months without these thoughts, and then they'd sneak up on him. Every time, he had to force them away. He wouldn't blame Jillian.

Meredith's face tightened as if she'd misinterpreted his silence. "Unless you think she wasn't intelligent enough to make that decision for herself."

"I certainly don't think that."

"Good." She unwrapped her silverware and set the

pieces precisely on the table. "Let me tell you, Zach Gilcroft, I know all about being responsible for a person's death—or rather two people's deaths—and you aren't even close."

⌒◦⌒

"What are you talking about?" Zach stared at her, eyes wide.

Meredith's cheeks got as hot as that time she had an allergic reaction to a face cream. "I— Never mind." Was she crazy? She should have kept her mouth shut.

The waitress slid Meredith's plate of burnt ends and onion rings in front of her, then served Zach's ribs and fries. "Oops. Forgot the slaw." She hurried away.

"Never mind?" Zach grabbed a fry and pointed it at Meredith. "You can't say something like that and not explain."

"Here we go." The waitress swooped back in and deposited a bowl of slaw beside each of their plates. Then she set down ketchup and two bottles of red barbecue sauce, one marked *Sweet*, the other *Hot*. "Flag me down if you need anything else."

Meredith took a big bite of burnt ends and gestured that her mouth was full.

"You're stalling."

Yep. Stalling and trying desperately to find a way out of this conversation. She chewed slowly and pulled out her phone, hoping that the radar showed a wide pink band of ice about to hit so they'd have to rush home. No such luck.

Zach squirted some ketchup near his fries and added a large pool of sweet sauce on the other side of the plate. Then he cut off one of the ribs and dipped it in the sauce.

He took a bite and sat back, chewing, watching her as if ready for the whole story.

She frowned and wiped her mouth. "Fine. I'll tell you, but only so you can see the difference between what you did and actually being responsible for someone's death."

The conversation wouldn't be pretty, and it would scuttle her foolish dreams that he might take her out again, but if it helped him get over his pain, she needed to tell him.

"Okay." She ran a hand over the paper napkin in her lap. "The summer after my sophomore year at Truman State, I was dating a guy who lived over in Miller's Junction. Ava went to the nine o'clock movie at the theater over there one night, and I was supposed to pick her up and bring her home. My phone was on silent and I lost track of time. She ended up calling home, getting Dad out of bed, and having him come get her."

"I thought both of your parents—"

"We don't know for sure, but we guess that Mom was afraid he'd get sleepy, so she went with him." She pressed her tongue against the roof of her mouth, the only way she'd learned to keep from crying. After a couple of seconds, she said the worst part quickly. "A trucker fell asleep at the wheel, crossed the yellow line, and crashed into them, killing them both. He wasn't even hurt."

"Oh, Meredith. How horrible."

She scrunched up her napkin in her lap and compressed it into a tiny ball. "It was. After I realized how late it was, I called my sister. When she didn't answer, I phoned home, and my aunt was there and told me what had happened."

And then she'd had to drive home.

Despite how she tried to steel herself against it, an all-too-familiar ache clenched her chest. An ache that felt like two giant hands, squeezing and twisting her heart and lungs into a ball as tight as she'd squeezed the napkin in her lap.

That drive had been so awful. So very, very awful. Aunt Ruby had wanted Meredith to wait, wanted to send Uncle Harris to pick her up. But after she learned what had happened, Meredith had felt a desperate need to be home as soon as possible. In the end, Ruby made her promise to drive the back way, not the highway, and Meredith had understood what Ruby didn't say, that if she took the highway, she'd go right past the remains of the wreck.

It might have been better if she had.

She'd seen wrecks along the highway. None of them was as horrific as what her mind had conjured up. The whole way home, she'd alternated between sobbing and gasping for air. Her hands had been shaking as she gripped the steering wheel. The road had blurred, and the oncoming headlights had been magnified by her tears.

Even now, all these years later, she hated that back road between Abundance and Miller's Junction. And she hated the highway route too, especially the area where the accident had occurred, near County Road 629. Pretty much, if there was a way to avoid it, she didn't go to Miller's Junction.

And if that night hadn't been painful enough, the guy she'd been dating, the whole reason she'd caused her parents' death, broke up with her a week later. Was it any wonder she'd been picky about who she dated after that?

She stared down, focusing on Zach's hands as he used

an entire napkin to wipe barbecue sauce off his fingers.

Then he reached across to take her hand.

She let out a shaky breath and sat there, silent, savoring the comfort and strength that seemed to flow from his hand into hers. Bit by bit, the past released its grip on her chest.

She straightened her shoulders. She hadn't meant to get so upset. This wasn't about her. It was about getting Zach to see his own past differently. She pulled her hand away, clasped her fingers together in her lap, and looked up at him. "Sorry about that. It just hits me sometimes."

Zach nodded slowly. "I know."

"Anyway, what I wanted to say was that your wife had a choice. What choice did my parents have when Ava needed to get home and they couldn't reach me?"

"What about the trucker?" Zach leaned closer. "Didn't he play a part?"

"If my parents' car hadn't been there, he might have hit a pothole, woken up, and swerved back into his own lane without a problem."

"I doubt it." Zach turned a French fry over in his ketchup, coating one end. "He had a choice. He was driving tired. He should have stopped for coffee. Or a nap."

She raised one eyebrow. "Maybe, but I think it's my fault. If it wasn't for my negligence, my folks would still be around for me. And for Ava."

Zach stopped suddenly, fry halfway to his mouth, and tilted his head to one side.

A large drip of ketchup hit his white dress shirt.

"I am such a klutz." He set the fry on his plate, pulled a napkin from the dispenser, and wiped his shirt. "Is that why you want to open a restaurant? To help your sister out of guilt?"

"No." It wasn't guilt. Helping Ava was her responsibility. And had been, ever since the funeral, ever since Meredith realized that Aunt Ruby could only do so much.

Zach said. "Does Ava blame you?"

"She acts like she doesn't, but she must, deep inside."

"Why? You're not really responsible for your parents' deaths."

Meredith's shoulders stiffened. It would be impolite and probably a waste of time to tell the man he was flat-out wrong.

"All right, call it a draw." Zach took a long drink of his soda. "I feel responsible for the deaths of Jillian and my son. You feel responsible for your parents'. At least we understand each other, probably better than anyone else can."

"True." Meredith picked up an onion ring. Not that she wanted Zach to feel as miserable as she sometimes did, but in a weird way it was nice to know that someone understood.

"A death can affect you in a lot of ways. Like no matter how hard I try, I can't seem to stop being overprotective of Hailey. These days she's desperate for me to buy her a horse. She's cleaned out a stall in our barn and been telling me how convenient it is that some vet works from her home, just two houses past you."

"Cathy Wainwright. She takes care of Duke."

Zach's lips pressed together.

Meredith was no mind reader, but she didn't think Hailey was getting a horse any time soon.

Zach ran a hand through his hair. "Even when I know

it frustrates her, I don't want her doing anything risky. I try to think things through logically and be reasonable, but I'm worried that I'll lose her too."

"Aw, Zach." Meredith sighed. "I'd be overprotective too, if I were you."

"Thanks. If I were you, I'd want to make things up to my sister."

She nodded.

He picked up another fry, moved it toward the ketchup, then—as if he'd remembered the drip on his shirt—stopped and ate it plain. "Hey, maybe we should talk about your business plan now."

Zach shifted his SUV into Park. The drive back to Meredith's house from Whole Hog had gone by so fast.

"Your ideas are brilliant." She patted her purse as she climbed out of the car. "I've got them all in here on the paper place mat."

A zing of pride sped through his chest, and he scrambled out. "Thanks. I was impressed with your ideas too, and your tenacity." He walked with her toward her farmhouse, having parked in her driveway, as if they had been on a date. Which they hadn't. He simply wanted to talk with her a few minutes longer. "Your goal of getting the second greenhouse operational so you can raise more capital is great. It's bound to impress the Small Business Administration."

"I love your suggestion about applying for a loan from them as a woman-owned business. One way or another, I'll help Ava reach her dreams and open a restaurant. But I will work on letting go of the guilt. What you said about the trucker made sense."

"Yeah. What you said made sense too." He didn't want to blame Jillian for what happened, but Meredith's convictions had made him feel better. It would be nice to think that Jillian's death wasn't his fault. That he wasn't a horrible person.

That he might even consider dating another woman.

One woman in particular.

Meredith beamed at him, then climbed her porch steps. "You know, I think we helped each other tonight."

"We did." He followed her up the steps. "I normally don't talk about what happened with Jillian, and I can't believe I told you, but you were easy to talk to. Maybe I somehow sensed that you'd understand."

"I do understand, and I felt like you understood me. Better than anyone."

Despite the chill in the air, warmth surrounded his heart. Who knew? Was there a reason he'd moved in next door to a person who'd gone through the same type of anguish that he had? Would spending time together help them heal?

Or was it simply that the longer he was around Meredith, the more he was attracted to her?

"Well." He touched her arm. "I guess I'll say goodnight."

But he didn't.

He stood there, staring at her.

As if he'd spent the last six years alone on a deserted island and now, after finally getting rescued and given someone to talk to, he didn't want the connection to end.

Which was ridiculous. He hadn't been alone. He'd had

work, and he'd done stuff with friends. He'd spent lots of time with Hailey. And rarely, very rarely, when it was almost required for a business event, he'd gone out with a woman, making it clear it was a one-time thing.

All that time, he'd thought he was fine.

He'd been wrong.

Now, it was as if his heart had been reconnected to his brain, and it was sending a signal, a blaring, insistent signal, that Stacey was right. He needed someone in his life.

Even for a guy like him, who lived in a world of fast deals and quick decisions, the connection he felt with Meredith after such a short time was surprising. The same thing had happened at the long-ago bonfire.

His mind drifted back to Jillian, and he swallowed. It didn't matter what was going through his brain. He needed to go home.

He edged back.

But his chest ached, protesting that he was moving in the wrong direction.

Almost without thinking, he took off his gloves and shoved them in his pocket. He slid one hand around Meredith's back, drew her closer, and threaded the other hand into her hair, resting it at the base of her scalp. The strands flowed over his fingers, just as silky as they looked.

Through their coats, he felt her chest rise and fall against his.

For a long moment he gazed down into her eyes, heart pounding as if he was back in high school and had never kissed a girl before. Those same self-doubts that ran through his mind at fifteen did another lap through his brain twenty years later. Should he kiss her? Did she want him to? Should he give her an awkward hug and go home?

Meredith snuggled closer and her lips parted slightly.

His own lips tingled in response. Logic left his brain, and he brought his lips to hers.

She pressed her warm lips to his.

A shiver of pleasure spread through him, and he kissed her again and again and again.

At last, when icy raindrops pelted the back of his legs, he pulled away. "Wow."

"Yeah." She blinked up at him. "Wow."

He drew in a deep breath, trying to restart his brain. "I'd better get home before the road is coated in ice."

She appeared dazed, as if she didn't quite remember what ice was, but she nodded.

He put his gloves back on, touched her arm once more, and then made his way down her already slick porch steps and to the door of his SUV.

Partly because of the ice, partly because of how stunned he felt, he drove the short distance to his house very slowly and carefully. He almost clicked opened the garage door, but remembered it was still jam-packed with boxes and stuff for the bathroom remodel, so he turned off the car in the driveway.

Somehow, he didn't slip once on the ice getting inside the house.

On the other hand, he might have already fallen.

On Meredith Lawson's porch.

Chapter Eight

Meredith poured a cup of coffee and set it on the kitchen table next to her laptop. Enough putting it off. She'd glanced out the window at the thick snow that had fallen after that brief bit of freezing rain. Brewed a fresh pot of coffee. Gotten out a notepad, found her favorite pen, and even—after a long hunt for the sharpener—sharpened a pencil. All to fill out an online form.

This was just a simple form from the Small Business Administration, but it seemed like a big deal. It seemed like *the* answer to saving Ava's dream of an organic restaurant.

Which was why she needed to get to work.

She sat down, straightened her shoulders, and turned on the laptop.

A log in the fireplace let out a pop, shooting up orange sparks, startling her and waking Duke. He rose from the rug in front of the fireplace, stretched, and walked through the doorway into the kitchen, stopping at Meredith's side to give her a chance to pet him.

A well-trained human, she rubbed his soft ears. "You're a handsome boy, aren't you?"

With a look of love and then a snuffle, he settled to the floor beside her, resting his head on the tops of her slippers.

Meredith gazed back at the fire. The real problem wasn't the SBA form. The problem was that even getting out the laptop to work on the form made her fidgety because it made her think about Zach.

Zach Gilcroft.

Who had—she squeezed her arms around herself like a teenager—kissed her.

Zach. Gilcroft. Had. Kissed. Her.

And, though she might be kidding herself, she really thought he wanted to kiss her again.

Swirls of happiness as light and pink and fluffy as cotton candy from the county fair filled her chest. What if he asked her out again?

And they started dating.

And it developed into a relationship and—

Wait a minute. She needed to use her brain. This was *Zach Gilcroft*. The guy who'd never called after they sat together at that bonfire years ago. The guy who was a super-successful entrepreneur. The guy who'd married a beauty queen.

No more daydreaming. She needed to focus on the SBA form.

Meredith opened her laptop and moved her cursor to the first blank.

Name:

Carefully, she typed in *Meredith Lawson*.

See? She could do this. This, not some romantic dream, was why fate had brought Zach into her life, to get her to apply for this loan.

A quick sip of coffee, and she tabbed over to the next blank.

She typed in her address. Then, as she put in her ZIP Code, a knock sounded on the kitchen door behind her.

Duke let out a woof and lurched out from under the table.

Meredith spun around.

Hailey waved through the glass.

She quickly saved her work and opened the door. "Hailey, come in."

"I shouldn't. Dad wants me to rush back and unpack another two boxes in my bedroom." She rolled her eyes. "Really, they could wait."

Duke wiggled closer to Hailey and nudged her leg.

She whispered something to him and patted his head. "But tonight Dad agreed that we can go sledding after it gets dark. I found an old sled over at Grandpa's, and Dad's out scouting a good place, probably that spot past the cedars, where there's that little hill."

Meredith knew exactly where Hailey meant. She and Ava had gone sledding there with their cousin, Jake, when they were kids, but— "In the dark?"

"Yeah. The forecast says all these clouds will clear out, and the moon is supposed to be full and really bright. He said I could invite you. Are you free? I'd really like you to come." Hailey looked up at her with huge, hopeful eyes. "Duke's invited too, of course."

Meredith's heart melted. How could she possibly say

no to this sweet girl?

And how could she refuse a chance to go sledding in the moonlight with Zach?

If she was completely honest with herself, she had to admit that she'd jump at any chance to spend time with him.

Scrubbing floors? She'd say yes. Cleaning toilets? Yes again. Shoveling manure? Even then—after perhaps a moment's hesitation—yes.

But *sledding* with Zach? Possibly even sharing a sled with him and having him wrap his arms around her to keep her steady? Falling into a snowbank with him? Brushing the snow off his face while the moon shone down on them like some old-fashioned romantic movie?

Yes! Yes! Yes!

"Sure, Hailey," Meredith said nonchalantly. "That sounds like fun."

"Yay! Just come over at nine." Hailey raced back across the yard toward her house.

"See you tonight!" Meredith took hold of Duke's collar and pulled him back inside. If she let him go, he'd follow Hailey all the way home, probably right into her bedroom. "Don't worry, boy, you'll get to see her again tonight."

She gave his ears a rub and went over to the kitchen table to close her laptop.

The form from the Small Business Administration would have to wait. It was time to come up with the perfect outfit for sledding.

～◦～

"This is it." Zach stood with Hailey and Meredith and pointed to the snowy hill sparkling before them in the moonlight.

"Excellent!" Hailey bounced up and down like she used to when she was younger. His girl was so cute, bundled in her turquoise coat and gloves and—because she couldn't find her matching hat—an old black knit cap of his. "This is great, Dad!"

Meredith, wearing a red coat and a red hat with a white pompom on the top, peered out into the night with almost the same look of childlike wonder and excitement as Hailey. As if she still found delight in the simple things in life. Which might be part of what made her so appealing.

Well, that and her big brown eyes. And the cute way her nose turned up. And those curves that, although now hidden by her coat, he remembered from the restaurant.

There was no denying it. He was definitely attracted to this woman.

And it wasn't only a physical thing. There was that childlike delight. Her resilient attitude when facing business challenges. The sweet way she interacted with Hailey, as if she really cared about his girl. Her kindness and understanding that let him talk about his past more easily than with anyone else. Somehow it all combined in a way that simply made him happier when he was with her.

He only hoped Hailey would like her as well.

Sledding seemed like a good start. He'd been surprised when Hailey suggested inviting Meredith to join them. He'd quickly realized the invitation was probably mostly for her dog, but still, he was secretly thrilled. He'd love it if Hailey could get to know Meredith and see how nice she was.

At the moment, though, Hailey was deeply engrossed

in a conversation with Duke, explaining how they didn't have snow back in Phoenix.

The hill, to be perfectly honest, wasn't that steep. Northern Missouri was fairly flat. Zach wasn't sure how fast their sleds would go. As predicted, though, the clouds had moved off, and the moon was full. With the way the moonlight reflected off the snow, seeing to steer wouldn't be a problem. And the air was crisp but quite comfortable for playing outside. A perfect night for sledding.

"You go first, Meredith." Hailey pointed to the two sleds. "Which one do you want?"

Pride welled up in Zach. Look at his girl, showing her good manners by letting their guest go first. He must have gotten a few things right as a dad.

Meredith looked at the purple saucer sled they had found at Dad's, then at the long, black plastic sled she'd brought. "I'm sticking with this one." She tapped the black sled. "Ava and I rode this thing a million times. I know how to handle it." She grinned and sat on the sled, bracing her feet against the plastic lip in front. "I just need to get"— she pushed at the ground, one hand on each side of the sled—"going."

"I can help with that." Zach leaned down and gripped the back of the sled. "Ready?"

She nodded and the white pompom on the top of her red knit cap bounced up and down. "Ready!"

He gave the sled a good push, and she zipped away, slowing at the base of the hill near a large oak.

"Me next, Dad!" Hailey was already positioned on the saucer sled. "But give me a harder push. I want to go faster."

"All right, you daredevil." He aimed the saucer to the left of both the oak and Meredith and gave Hailey a running push. The purple saucer slid down the hill and spun once at the bottom.

Meredith waited, halfway up the hill, then walked up the rest of the way with Hailey. It seemed the two of them were getting along well and Hailey was having a wonderful time. Exactly what Zach wanted. In his perfect world, Hailey would be happy all the time. And have no objections when Zach brought up the fact that he wanted to date Meredith.

Soon Meredith and Hailey reached the top of the hill, and Zach took a turn on the black sled, gliding down the hill next to Hailey, who maneuvered the saucer sled like a pro, thanks to vacations they'd taken at ski resorts.

Again and again the three of them sledded down the hill until the temperature began to drop.

"How about one more turn for each of us?" Zach asked.

"Let's race!" Hailey said, sitting on the black sled. "Meredith and me against you, Dad."

"Me on the saucer? My legs are too long."

They ignored his protests. Within seconds, they were positioned on the black sled with Meredith in the back, arms stretched out, ready to push off, and Hailey in the front, holding the rope.

"Better hurry, Zach." Meredith laughed. "You don't want to lose to a couple of girls, do you?"

He gave her a look of mock offense, scrunched himself up to fit on the saucer, and pushed off.

"We didn't say go!" Hailey yelled after him.

"Don't worry, we'll still win!" Meredith shouted. "Lean back, Hailey. We'll go faster."

They whooshed past him, squealing as they flew down the hill.

Zach pushed off again with both hands, shoving hard against the snow, but the saucer sled was so small that he couldn't distribute his weight properly. He wobbled down the hill, a failure for men everywhere.

"The champions!" Meredith yelled. She stood, grasped Hailey's hand, and held it high.

"Meredith Lawson, didn't anyone ever tell you that it's rude to brag?" He climbed off the saucer, scooped a handful of snow, and packed it tight.

"You wouldn't dare." She took a step backward.

He chuckled. And threw.

The snowball hit her straight in the chest, exploding with such force that snow sprayed up in her face.

Her eyes flew wide, and he burst out laughing.

And kept laughing as Meredith and Hailey instantly formed a team and attacked, pelting him with snowballs.

There was no need, no need at all, to worry about the two of them getting along.

"I should head home." Meredith got up from Zach's kitchen table, walked to the back door, and slid on her boots.

"Are you sure?" Zach followed her and placed a hand on her upper arm. "I can fix us more cocoa."

A zing of electricity hit her, the same reaction she'd had repeatedly since they came inside from sledding. When his blue eyes twinkled as Hailey pulled out the store-bought cookies. When his muscles tightened beneath his navy Henley shirt as he lifted a gallon of milk out of the fridge to mix into instant cocoa. When his eyes met hers as Hailey went upstairs to shower after their snack and left the two of them alone.

Everything the man did seemed to affect her.

Clearly, she'd had far too much fun playing in the snow with him.

Oh, sledding in the moonlight had sounded wonderful at first, but she'd let herself get carried away.

In spite of what she might wish for, in spite of the kiss last night, nothing had changed. She was still plain old Meredith Lawson. Zach was rich, successful, and drop-dead handsome. If she wasn't careful, she'd get her heart crushed like she had at eighteen.

She grabbed her coat from a hook by the door and pulled it on. "Thanks for the offer, but I should go. It was really nice of you and Hailey to include me tonight."

That was something else to remember. Hailey had been the one to invite her, not Zach. She and Zach were neighbors, nothing more.

He took a step closer. "So, can I take you out on a real date?"

She fumbled with the last button on her coat, totally missing the buttonhole. A real date? "Are you sure? I mean, I saw a photo of your wife. She looked like a model. I'm just—"

"Adorable." He brushed a hand down her cheek. "Absolutely adorable."

Her heart sped.

"I should have called you years ago, after we talked so

long at that bonfire, but I was an idiot at nineteen. I listened to my buddies when they told me to only date cheerleaders." He gave a rueful shrug. "It took a while, but I grew up and got a brain. And I really like you."

His words repeated in her mind as if they were spelled out by fireworks, each with its own explosion.

He. Really. Liked. Her.

The zings of attraction she'd experienced before were mere ripples compared to the wave of emotion that hit her now. Her entire body felt light, as if she might float away on a river of happiness.

Zach Gilcroft wanted to date her. It was incredible. It was fantastic. It was too wonderful to be true and—

His eyebrows bunched together.

Her heart screeched to a halt. Why were his eyebrows drawing together? Why did he look uncomfortable? Had he realized, as soon as he asked her out, that he wanted to take it back?

He ran a hand through his hair, looked down, and blew out a long breath. "I'm not good at this. I don't normally date, except for business functions." He looked back up at her. "I really think this could be something special, but I need to talk to Hailey first."

Hailey? The only obstacle was that he loved his daughter and wanted to talk to her first? Meredith's heart leapt back to top speed as fast as an Olympic athlete off the starting blocks. Was there any way for Zach to be more endearing or for her to be more attracted to him?

He slid an arm around her waist. "So, unless Hailey seems upset about the idea, how about dinner next weekend? Maybe someplace nice in Kansas City?"

Dinner. He was asking her to dinner. Not a working dinner at Whole Hog Barbecue but a real date, a fancy dinner in Kansas City. Which meant she needed a response other than gasping for breath. "I'd like that. Let me know what she says."

"She's gonna say yes, Meredith." Zach pulled her close. "It's a formality. She likes you. I'm sure of it. Any woman who can pummel her dad with snowballs the way you did…"

He chuckled, and his breath danced over Meredith's lips.

The room suddenly seemed ten degrees warmer.

"I did get you pretty good," she whispered.

"I'll call you in the morning." His lips hovered above hers. "To tell you what Hailey says."

"That sounds great." If her life depended on it, she couldn't have moved away.

He ran a hand down her back, and in less than a second, their bodies melted into one.

Every one of her nerve endings was electrified. She gazed up into his eyes, unable to escape their blue-gray depths.

Slowly, very slowly, he brought his lips toward hers, hovering a fraction of an inch away.

A tortured bliss engulfed her until at last—at long, long last—he kissed her.

She slid her fingers into his hair, drew him closer, and drank in kisses that tasted of cocoa. Cocoa…and possibilities.

Finally, knees weak, she stepped back. She drew in a shaky breath and nudged a snoring Duke with her toe to wake him.

Unable to speak, she waved and slipped out the door.

Above, the moon shone down at her, its face of mountains and craters quirked into a tender smirk. She could almost imagine what it might be thinking.

Had she really believed she stood a chance tonight, guarding her heart against Zach's kisses and the incredible power of moonlight?

Had she really thought she wouldn't fall in love?

Foolish human.

Chapter Nine

"Here we are." Zach pulled up to valet parking.

Meredith's stomach tightened as she read the name over the door. The Table was one of the most expensive restaurants in Kansas City. The place Ava had worked for four years. And the last place Meredith wanted to eat dinner.

She'd done so well when they started the drive from Abundance. She'd told herself that the sleeveless black dress Ava had talked her into buying last summer was elegant enough for a Saturday evening in the city. She'd reminded herself that Zach really liked her. She'd even replayed their conversation from the morning after they'd gone sledding when he'd phoned with the news that Hailey "was totally chill" with the idea of them dating.

For the last half hour of the drive to Kansas City, she'd been happily chatting with Zach, and, every once in a while, trying to get him to slip and tell her his big secret—

the name of the play they were seeing after dinner. She'd been having fun.

Until now.

The valet opened her door. Which she thought meant that she was supposed to get out. It wasn't as if she'd ever used valet parking before.

And it wasn't as if she wanted to set foot in The Table.

Should she say something to Zach?

No. She'd sound whiny and difficult, and she'd have to admit one of the failings of her business.

She grabbed her purse and climbed out of his car.

He got out on the driver's side, looking incredibly handsome in a charcoal-gray suit. More handsome than she could remember a man looking in real life. To be honest, the only time she saw men as hot as Zach, wearing clothes that fit so well, was in a movie or when she read *People* magazine at the hair salon.

He handed his keys to the valet and slipped him some cash as calmly as if he used valet parking every weekend.

Which maybe he did, back in Phoenix.

She peered through the restaurant windows at the elegant diners, people who were probably discussing stock options and tax shelters and vacation homes while they enjoyed the restaurant's signature dry-aged beef and fresh seafood.

Was there anything that could make the differences between her and Zach more obvious?

In Abundance, she could—if she let her heart take control—see herself with him. Not here. Not at The Table. Not where he'd be the successful entrepreneur, and she'd be the failure.

If only she'd found out where they were going when Zach asked what type of food she liked.

"Ready?" He offered his arm.

She squashed down the tension in her chest and slipped her arm through his.

Two minutes later, the maître d' had found their reservation, and they were seated in softly upholstered chairs at a table with a snowy white cloth, a trio of flickering candles, and a vase of peach rosebuds. A basket of fresh-baked bread sat between the two of them, filling the air with its yeasty scent. The waitress gave them menus, filled their water goblets, and told them about three entrée specials.

As soon as she walked away, Zach leaned in. "Are you okay?"

"Sure." Her voice cracked. "Doesn't that bread smell delicious?" She pulled a slice from the basket, buttered it, and took a bite, expecting her nerves to render it flavorless. Instead, the rich tang of the sourdough melded with the sweet, creamy butter, creating a contrast that delighted every taste bud in her mouth.

Zach's brow furrowed. "If you don't like this place, we can go somewhere else. I only picked it because my sister had heard it was good."

"I'm sure it will be delicious. This bread certainly is." She forced a smile to her lips and opened the menu. Her eyes immediately fell to the list of salads.

Which didn't even mention the word *microgreens*. Odd. She'd thought the same guy that got the contract for the Columbia restaurant would supply The Table.

"Meredith, what's going on? You said you liked steak

and seafood. Reading the menu shouldn't make you look so wounded."

Her shoulders fell. So much for her ability to conceal her feelings. "I used to sell microgreens to a restaurant in Columbia that's run by the same executive chef as this place."

"Oh." Zach closed his menu. "What happened?"

"The kitchen manager called me a year ago. She said they had replaced me with another vendor."

"Why?"

"I have no idea. I asked, but Celeste, the manager, was really dismissive. She acted as if I should know what I'd done wrong. I—" Her chest tightened, and she raised her menu. "Can we discuss something else? The executive chef just came out to talk to a table a few feet behind you."

"Really, we can leave," Zach said in a loud whisper. "There are lots of restaurants on the Plaza."

"Not ones where we can get served fast enough without a reservation before whatever play we're seeing starts at eight." Even the cheaper places at the Plaza were crowded on a Saturday night.

"Meredith Lawson!" The voice boomed out from behind Zach.

She lowered her menu. The executive chef, Marcus, was walking right toward her, the white jacket of his uniform gleaming, his small, curled mustache reminding her, as always, of the 1920s.

"I've been meaning to call you." Marcus took her hand and squeezed it between both of his. "How wonderful that you're here tonight. I owe you such an apology. May I"—he glanced from her to Zach—"may I interrupt for five minutes?"

Zach raised an eyebrow and gave Meredith an encouraging nod when Marcus wasn't looking.

"Sure." Under the table, discreetly hidden by the tablecloth, she nervously ran her hands over the skirt of her dress.

Marcus drew up a chair and set a small plate before them that he'd made appear from out of nowhere. "Gouda fritters with a sweet mustard sauce, my new favorite starter."

"They smell delicious." Zach dipped one in the sauce, popped it in his mouth, and let out a soft groan.

Marcus's chest swelled, and he turned to Meredith, speaking much more quietly. "I recently let Celeste go."

Meredith's hands froze, wads of her skirt clasped between her fingers.

"I learned she was taking kickbacks from certain vendors and letting greed take priority over the quality of the food at my restaurant down in Columbia. In the course of our rather heated discussion, I learned that we stopped ordering microgreens from you because you weren't a part of her scheme, not—as she told me at the time—because you delivered a shipment that was wilted and refused to replace it."

That was what had been going on? "I never—I mean, if there was any problem, I would have brought you a new shipment but—"

"But there was never a problem in the first place, was there?" Marcus gave a bitter smile. "Your produce was always exceptional, far nicer than anything I got elsewhere. I should have seen her lie for what it was, but..." He clenched his fists, then spread his fingers wide, as if releasing his anger. "Is there any way you can forgive me? Any way you can provide me with produce again?"

"Oh, um—" Meredith's brain felt as though it were exploding. She glanced across the table at Zach.

"Zach Gilcroft." He reached out and shook Marcus's hand. "These fritters are exceptional. From what I've seen, Meredith's produce seems in pretty high demand, but I do think she's considering expanding her production in the next year."

"You are?" Marcus turned back to her. "As soon as you're able, I'll put in a regular order of double what we were buying before. I'd love to have you supply both the Columbia restaurant and The Table. In the meantime, I'll take whatever you can spare, if you'll dare to do business with me again."

With effort, she refrained from shrieking and jumping up and down like an eight-year-old. "I'd be happy to. I'm not sure what we'd do about delivery for The Table. It's more than two hours from my greenhouse to here. I can keep it cool, but—"

Marcus waved her concern aside. "I would be happy to cover a delivery fee."

"Meredith, don't forget about the price increase you're planning." Zach gave Marcus an apologetic look. "Totally unavoidable. The only way to increase production is to put in a sprinkler system."

"Say no more." Marcus flicked his fingers at Zach's words. "The supplier Celeste switched to started out cheaper than you, but gradually raised his rates until we were paying twenty percent more, and his produce wasn't nearly the quality of yours."

Meredith's nerves bounced inside her skin. "After I get the second greenhouse working, not including the delivery fee, I can supply what you need at—" Was she really going to negotiate for more than market rate?

From across the table, Zach leaned forward, nodding slightly.

She drew in a deep breath. "At only fifteen percent over what you were paying before."

Marcus kissed her hand. "You are an angel. I'll call Monday to see how soon you can supply the full order, and to beg for what you can give me in the meantime."

"Thank you."

Marcus called over their waitress. "I want you to take the very best care of this table tonight. Their meal—anything they want—is on me."

Meredith raised a hand to her chest. "My goodness. Thank you."

Marcus apologized to Zach for the interruption, suggested he order a steak that Meredith had spotted as the most expensive entrée on the menu, and thanked her again before sailing back toward the kitchen.

"Wow." Zach leaned back, chuckling. "I didn't realize I was going out to dinner with a celebrity tonight."

"I can't believe that just happened. Fifteen percent over what he was paying before."

"He was grateful to get that deal. You must grow extremely nice produce." Zach's eyes shone. "I'm so proud of you. You're an amazing woman, Meredith Lawson."

Tingles radiated through her chest and down her arms. Zach Gilcroft was proud of her.

And he'd called her amazing. This night was too good

to be true.

He slid the appetizer plate toward her. "Now try one of these fritters before I eat them all."

"Are you sure you don't want anything?" Zach gestured to the theater's concession stand, which was doing a booming business during intermission. The air was filled with the aroma of roasted nuts, and a discreet sign overhead announced that soft drinks and wine were also available.

"Thanks, but I'm still too full from dinner." Meredith slid her evening bag under her arm. "That seven-layer chocolate torte was really rich."

"It was."

"I'm glad we split it." She rested a hand on his sleeve. "This show is such a fun surprise. I love Rodgers and Hammerstein, and *Oklahoma* is my favorite. How did you know?"

"I didn't. I just picked it because it's about an adorable farm girl."

Meredith's eyelashes fluttered down and her cheeks grew pinker.

Warmth filled his chest. She was so sweet, with no idea how lovely she was.

Or how much he liked her.

When they weren't together, he was planning the next time he would see her. If he'd already made plans with her, he was looking forward to them. Last week, he'd gotten so wrapped up in staring out the window at her house and greenhouses that he'd missed a scheduled call with Cliff. Yesterday, he'd found all the songs of *Oklahoma* and played them on his phone, wondering which one she'd like best.

This morning, he'd woken up, realized that tonight was their date in Kansas City, and bolted out of bed, as if it might make the evening arrive sooner.

He had it bad.

If someone had asked him before Christmas, he'd have sworn he'd be single for the rest of his life. The more he was with Meredith, though, the more that opinion changed.

"Oh, look." Meredith waved to someone across the lobby. "I think that's Danielle. I haven't seen her since I was at Truman State."

The blond woman waved back, took the man beside her by the arm, and hurried over.

A moment later, Zach and the man, Chad, were discussing the upcoming season for the Kansas City Royals.

Meredith and Danielle, after letting out a few squeals and hugging each other like long-lost siblings, appeared to be telling each other every detail of their lives since they were sophomores in college.

"You did?" Meredith's words rose with excitement, and she laid a hand on Danielle's arm. "Photos, now!"

Danielle let out a laugh and pulled out her phone. "She's eleven months old. This is our first big night out since she was born." She tapped her phone and held it toward Meredith.

Meredith took the phone and her face softened. "Oh, she's gorgeous." There was a note of reverence in her voice, and her eyes were misty. "Are there more pictures?"

An icy frisson rushed through Zach's chest.

"Sure." Danielle touched the screen. "Just scroll

through. The whole camera roll is pretty much one baby photo after another."

Meredith gazed at the phone, oohing and ahing again and again.

With each expression of delight, Zach's heart constricted more tightly.

How could he have been so stupid?

He should have realized that Meredith loved kids. Look how nurturing she was with Hailey. She was born to be a mom. If he built a future with her, she was bound to want a child of her own.

She'd want to get pregnant.

Pregnant. The word hovered in his mind like a churning storm cloud.

And then heat crashed into his chest, and he couldn't hold the anger back any longer.

He'd fought it for so long. Told himself it was wrong to be mad at a woman he loved, a woman who'd died carrying his child. Told himself her death was his fault, that he was the man, he should have protected her. Told himself that Hailey might pick up on his feelings if he let himself be mad at Jillian, and that it would be unspeakable to turn a child against her dead mother.

But no matter what he told himself, the feelings hadn't gone away.

He was angry that Jillian had talked him into trying to have another baby. Angry that she'd insisted she'd be fine and then wasn't. And most of all, angry because he'd trusted that she would put their marriage and Hailey as her top priorities, and she hadn't.

She'd chased after another child because he and Hailey

weren't enough to make her happy.

Which shredded everything he'd believed about their relationship into confetti. Worthless, disposable confetti.

That was why he felt a sense of duty, not sorrow, as he hung Jillian's photos in the new house, why he'd gone six years without having another relationship, and why the idea of Meredith one day getting pregnant upset him.

Now, as if he'd been hit by a jolt of lightning, he realized he couldn't really trust any woman, not even Meredith. Not when it came to babies.

And how could he have a relationship if he couldn't trust?

Chad shifted position, coming into Zach's field of vision. "...if the Royals are going to make it to the playoffs this year, that's the key," Chad said. "Don't you agree?"

"Uh, yeah." Whatever. For all Zach knew, he might have just agreed that the team needed to replace their uniforms with ballet tutus. He turned toward Meredith. He'd had all the polite conversation he could handle. "We'd better take our seats."

"Oh, sure." Meredith hugged Danielle once more. "Call me. We have to get together so I can meet your daughter. She's just darling."

Zach mumbled goodbye to the couple and sped Meredith to their seats, barely making it before the lights dimmed.

Chapter Ten

Compared with many of her friends from Abundance, Meredith was at ease in city traffic, comfortable as a passenger or the driver. Before she got her license, her dad had made her practice navigating all over Kansas City. Back then, with both Mom and Dad working the greenhouse, sparing a person to run an order to Kansas City once a week wasn't that difficult. After Dad's driving lessons, she'd taken over those deliveries in the summers.

Of course, back then her family hadn't been growing microgreens. Those days it had been mostly heirloom tomatoes.

Trends in produce might have changed, but basic driving skills hadn't.

Tonight, though, getting out of Kansas City was making her nervous, and she wasn't even driving. She was, however, well-aware of Zach's tension.

He gripped the wheel tightly, gaze never leaving the road.

For some reason the streets around the theater had been extremely crowded, far more so than could be accounted for by the audience from *Oklahoma* heading home. In addition, although it was only early March, summer road repair seemed to have already begun. Many streets were blocked off or reduced to one lane.

To make matters worse, once they'd gotten on the highway headed north, the road seemed to be populated with "an exceptionally high percentage of stupid," as Ava said she sometimes encountered in Atlanta. Drivers swerved across four lanes of traffic at once, forgot their cars had turn signals, and cut in and out of traffic at thirty miles over the speed limit.

Even so, Zach had lived in Phoenix. City driving wasn't a challenge he geared up for with extra coffee like she did. It was something he did every day.

And he hadn't seemed tense driving while they were on their way into Kansas City. She'd seen real pleasure on Zach's face as his car responded to his control. Now, as his car's engine gave a throaty hum as he passed a slower vehicle, his face remained grim.

No matter how bad the other drivers were tonight in Kansas City, they weren't the problem.

As she thought back over the evening, she realized that the tightness of his jawline, the long periods of uncomfortable silence, and the way he responded to her questions with curt replies had all started before they got in the car. She just hadn't noticed because she'd been having such a great time. Now, she peered out at the headlights pouring toward them across the median and twisted the tip of one glove between her fingers. If she wasn't mistaken, the problem had started during intermission. Had Danielle's husband said something that made Zach mad? Meredith had never met him before tonight, but Danielle was so nice, it was hard to picture her married to a jerk.

Or had she herself done something? Said something?

She didn't remember anything out of the ordinary.

No longer cold from the short walk through the theater's parking garage, she tapped the button to reduce the temperature of her seat heater. It had more than done its job.

If only there was a button to warm up the atmosphere between her and Zach.

But there wasn't, so she was going to have to broach the matter head on.

She waited until they were out of the city on the road headed east toward Abundance, then looked over at him.

Still brooding.

Just as she'd suspected, his mood had nothing to do with the traffic or the stupid drivers in the city. The road was almost entirely theirs.

"Hey," she said, trying to keep her voice light. "Is something wrong?"

He jerked his head toward her, gave a forced smile, and turned back to the road. "No. All good."

She sank down in her seat. The man had been married. Hadn't he learned the value of communication? "Are you sure? Because ever since intermission, you've seemed…" What was the least insulting way to put it? "On edge."

"I don't want to talk about it."

"We've got quite a drive before we get back to Abundance. It's an awfully long time for me to sit here in silence with you over there being prickly."

"I am *not* being prickly."

"He said in a tone as prickly as a porcupine." She sniffed.

No reply. Just a palpable wave of stress from the driver's side of the vehicle.

Okay, that comment about the porcupine was immature on her part. Not exactly showing good communication skills, but—

"I thought I'd dealt with everything related to my grief six years ago, but I haven't." Zach's words burst out, like water breaching a dam. "At first, I was so busy, taking care of Hailey and being strong for her. Then I guess I just kept busy as a way to avoid thinking about it." He glanced over at Meredith and then jerked his head back to stare at the road. "But I don't do well with babies, okay? Seeing you so excited about your friend's baby made me nervous."

"Oh." Heavens, she'd never even thought of that. "Zach, I'm so sorry." She rested a hand on his arm and felt the bunched muscles beneath his coat. Talk about insensitive. When she and Danielle were talking about that darling little one, Arabella, she should have realized that it might remind Zach of the baby he and his wife had lost. The poor man, still grieving after losing his wife and son six years ago and—

Wait a minute. Zach didn't say it made him sad. He said it made him nervous.

That was weird. If Danielle had been pregnant, Meredith could see how that might have made Zach nervous to be around her, but Arabella was already born. "You don't need to worry, Zach. Danielle didn't mention a single problem related to her health or the baby's, other than teething, and I'm pretty sure that's perfectly normal."

Zach blew out a heavy breath. "It's not your friend I'm worried about. When the two of you talked about babies, it made me realize that I hadn't thought through what it might mean if we kept seeing each other, if you one day wanted a child."

The air in her lungs was gone. Evaporated. Meredith pulled her shaking hand back from his arm and tried to appear as if she was studying the highway.

Good grief.

She'd admitted to herself that she was crazy about Zach. And she knew he lived in a world where deals were made fast and loved that part of his job. Still, she hadn't put together the fact that his brain worked at that high speed in all areas of his life, hadn't dreamed that he might have fallen for her as quickly as she'd fallen for him, or that he might already be picturing the two of them being married and her having a baby.

A baby.

She raised a hand to her chest. Her with a baby...

Zach flicked on his blinker and passed an old pickup that was creeping down the highway with one taillight missing. His motions were steady, his speed controlled, but the pain still radiated out.

No wonder. If they did stay together, if they one day got married—she paused a moment to cross her fingers—he'd probably be terrified that she'd get pregnant and he'd lose both her and the baby.

On the other hand, if she promised never to have children, would that be fair to her? Would she feel that she'd missed out? Would she be satisfied if her world consisted of Zach and Hailey?

Meredith stared ahead at the highway, watching the lines on the road appear to unfurl under the headlights. This decision mattered. She couldn't make a promise and change her mind later. The issue was too crucial to Zach.

No matter how long she pondered it, though, she came back to the same conclusion, the same certainty. If she got to a place where she and Zach were getting married, if she was going to have a future with him and Hailey, she wouldn't need anything more. Oh, babies were adorable, but not worth risking her life for. This decision didn't seem like a sacrifice. She knew that for some women, this decision would be difficult, something they agonized over, but for her, it seemed easy.

"Zach." She spoke softly and rested her hand on his arm.

He looked over at her, his eyes full of pain.

"If we were ever to—" She stopped. She couldn't actually use the word *married*. It was too soon, no matter where Zach's brain had raced. "If I was ever to, um, be in a relationship where the issue came up, I wouldn't want to have a baby unless the doctor assured both me and, um, the guy involved that it would be safe." Okay, that was convoluted. If they were actually going to communicate, she couldn't pretend this situation was hypothetical. She needed to speak directly. "If that was us, I couldn't bear to put you through nine months of worry."

"I couldn't ask that of you."

"You're not asking. I'm offering." She squeezed his arm. "I never was one of those girls who loved to play house and who chose my future children's names when I was in elementary school. It just wasn't me. If the doctor said getting pregnant was dangerous, I wouldn't want to do it. No offense to Jillian, but that seems foolish."

"It didn't seem foolish to her."

"Well, it does to me. Why would I want to take a chance of missing out on time with you and with Hailey? It makes a lot more sense to stay alive and enjoy a life with you. The two of you would more than fill my heart."

Suddenly, the car slowed, and Zach flicked on his blinker.

He turned off the highway onto an unmarked gravel road, parked, and looked her in the eyes.

A highway light shone dimly through the windows, and his jaw, his eyes, and even his shoulders relaxed.

"Thank you," he whispered. He pulled her into his arms and held her close. "I know this has been a strange conversation, but I'm so glad we had it." He brushed her hair back and gazed into her eyes. "And I'm so glad you're in my life, Meredith."

Her heart swelled. "I'm glad you're in my life, Zach." And she was glad their conversation had eased his pain.

He kissed her, held her for a long moment, and restarted the engine. "I guess we better get back to Abundance. Somebody might want to drive on this side road." He pulled back onto the highway, which stretched before them, straight and smooth.

No traffic. No construction.

No obstacles that would stand in the way of their relationship.

From here on, they shouldn't have any problems at all.

Chapter Eleven

Zach ran a knife through the tape across the top of the packing box, popped it open, and transferred the first handful of hanging files to his bottom desk drawer. If all went well, by the end of the day he'd have his home office, also known as the new Midwestern branch of Sunburst Energy, squared away. His desk would be clear, the tower of boxes that had been taunting him from the corner for the past two weeks would be unpacked, and the snarl of cords from his hastily set up electronics would be neatly aligned.

All things he should have done earlier, but he'd been busy.

Busy going out to lunch with his sister. Busy helping Hailey settle in. And well, yeah, busy getting to know his new neighbor.

But those were all good things.

Outside his office window, the sky was a vivid blue, with only a few small cirrus clouds off to the west. A day that—although not as profitable as a bright day in summer—would produce enough megawatt hours to make him smile. If the solar panels were already installed, Sunburst Energy would be making money.

Already the move to Abundance had helped Hailey. No more tears, no more door-slamming, no more acting as if every hour she spent on earth was painful. She'd even tried out for the school play and gotten the small, nonspeaking role she wanted.

And although Zach's date Saturday with Meredith hadn't gone exactly as he'd expected, it had turned out well in the end. It was incredible to think that after all those years alone since Jillian died, he'd found a woman who was not only cute and fun and but also great with his daughter. A woman who understood him and was sensible about risk. A woman would truly value a relationship with him and Hailey.

A woman he could trust.

Such a blessing. Add the fact that he'd talked for hours with Meredith, either in person or on the phone, every day since their date in Kansas City five days ago. Time had flown during every conversation, and he saw a real future for their relationship.

This move to Missouri was working out so well and—

His phone buzzed.

He tapped the screen to answer the call on speaker. "Hey, Cliff. How are things in Phoenix?"

"Abysmal. Did you read the email from Joe Webster?"

Zach's stomach tensed. "No." He moved the box he'd been unpacking to the floor, sat down, and booted up his computer. "I checked my email earlier, but—"

"He's decided not to invest."

"He was on board last week."

"Not anymore, and we can't raise a stink without risking his investment in the project in Nevada."

Zach logged in, found the email from Joe, and scanned it. His stomach twisted tighter. "So without his investment we're overextended by"—he ran the numbers in his head—"half a million?"

"Closer to three quarters," Cliff said.

Zach stood and walked across the room, arms wrapped over his gut, gazing out at the land where he'd pictured rows of solar panels.

Cold air seeped in through the single-pane windows. How had Meredith's aunt and uncle lived here for years without replacing them? Decent windows would have paid for themselves in energy savings. If he hadn't bought the house so fast, he could have negotiated new windows into the final price.

Downstairs, another thud sounded from the construction, followed by the whine of a power saw. If he hadn't been in such a rush to get here, he could have had the renovation completed before they moved in.

And all the sunshine in the world wouldn't help if his company couldn't afford the solar panels to capture it because they'd lost Joe's investment. Argh. The house, the investors. Everywhere he turned he saw evidence that he'd moved too fast.

But fast was the way he worked. Fast was what had made him a success. A guy didn't succeed in this business if he spent hours dithering around. Investors wanted big returns, and big returns meant cutting-edge tech and big risk.

Maybe fast wasn't the problem though. Maybe the problem was focus.

All that time he'd spent with Meredith had been time that he should have been working. He could have gotten this project farther along and been able to show Joe that his investment was going to pay off. He could have prevented this disaster.

He returned to his desk and skimmed the email again. "Do you think there's any way to get Joe back on board? What if one of us called him?"

"I just did." Cliff let out a sigh. "No go."

Zach stared at the tower of boxes in the corner, full of files of previous projects.

If there was one thing he'd learned from those projects, it was that no matter what, he had to keep trying. Success wasn't a matter of luck, it was a numbers game. The more times you tried, the more likely you were to win.

He sat up taller. "Okay, then. I'll get to work. I'll run over to see my sister. She's a real estate agent here in town, and I bet she's got some photos we can use to update the prospectus, give it more appeal."

"I'll start making some calls," Cliff said.

"Thanks, pal. One way or another, we'll get some new money into this project."

Because of all the ventures Zach had worked on over the years, this one was the most important. He was not moving away from Abundance. He was not taking Hailey back to Phoenix, where he knew she'd be even unhappier than before. And he was not leaving Meredith.

⸻

Meredith dumped the rest of Thursday's mail on the

kitchen table, took a pair of scissors from the drawer, and carefully opened the squishy, bubble-wrapped package from the seed company. Three large packets slid out—a colorful radish mix, some purple-leaf basil, and a rainbow combination of chard and beets.

A burst of excitement shot through her. She couldn't wait to start planting the new seeds. She just knew Marcus would love that chard and beet combo. And, thanks to the guys who'd worked all day yesterday and finished up this morning, she'd be planting them in the newly repaired greenhouse. Her business was growing exactly as she'd hoped. She stepped out the kitchen door, snapped a photo of the repaired greenhouse, then came back in, filled a glass of water, and sat at the kitchen table to send the photo to Ava.

Less than a minute later, the phone rang.

Meredith tapped the button to answer, set the phone on speaker, and put it on the table in front of her.

"The second greenhouse is fixed already?" Ava's voice bubbled with excitement.

"It is. I've got the heater running full blast to get it warmed up." Meredith arranged the new seed packets on the table behind the phone, neatly propping them in a line against the rest of the mail. "Step one in the plan to raise more capital, get a restaurant for you, and finally make up for what I did to Mom and Dad."

Ava didn't reply.

Unease squiggled through Meredith's stomach. She shouldn't have worded things quite that way. "I'm really excited about the restaurant, Ava. You're going to be a fabulous chef."

"Yeah, I'm excited about what I'm learning in culinary school." But Ava didn't sound excited. She sounded annoyed. "When are you going to get it through your head that you are not responsible for Mom and Dad's dying?"

"I—"

"It was an accident. You've got to see that, Meredith."

"I do, but I still think that accident never would have happened if I'd done what I said I would and picked you up." Meredith swept her hand across the table, scooping up the seed packets, no longer interested in admiring them.

"You lost track of time. Big deal. On the scale of dumb stuff that kids do, that barely registers. I did things that were far more stupid and careless, even after Mom and Dad died, when you had to deal with it. And remember Christine Beasley."

Christine Beasley? Meredith set the seed packets on the table. "What about her?" Christine had gone to school with Ava, but they hadn't been close friends, and she hadn't been involved the night of the accident.

"She was wild in high school, wrecked four cars in three years. Her parents were always having to come get her out of one mess or another. If there was ever someone who was irresponsible, it was her. Yet her parents are alive and well, and she eventually got all that rebellion out of her system and became a youth minister. Having a teenager who makes a mistake doesn't mean a person has to die." Ava sucked in a breath, and then spoke loudly, each word emphatic. "It. Was. An. Accident."

Meredith didn't say anything.

"Why can't you accept that it wasn't your fault?" Ava yelled.

Meredith's chest tightened. "I— I—"

"I never fully realized how messed up your brain is. You know, if you're only helping with the restaurant out of guilt, I don't want to pursue it."

Meredith's pulse sped. "Ava, it's more than that. I want you to be happy."

"No, you don't. You want to ease your guilt, but don't you see that you won't? You raised me. You're helping to pay for culinary school. You sacrificed again and again for me. And you still feel guilty. I don't want it anymore. I don't want you sacrificing for me. Do you really believe that makes me happy?"

"But—"

"I'm done. Forget about the restaurant. Forget about making things up to me. We're even. You've paid your debt. I don't need my own restaurant. I certainly don't need to live in Abundance. I can get a job as a chef somewhere else, and I'll be a lot better off."

The line went dead, and the words *Call Ended* appeared on Meredith's phone.

For a second, she sat, no different from before. Her pulse slightly elevated, her chest tight.

And then Ava's words, and all that they meant, came crashing in.

The base of her throat constricted. Her heart wrenched. And her chest caved in on itself. What had she done? In one short phone call she'd destroyed the whole plan for the two of them working together. Now she could never make up for what she'd done, and she'd totally messed up her relationship with her sister.

Numbly, not sure what else to do, she picked up the

seed packets and walked out the door toward the greenhouses.

Several minutes later, Hailey entered the newly repaired greenhouse and waved. "Hey, Meredith."

Meredith jerked her head toward the door. She'd forgotten all about Hailey coming by.

The girl dumped her backpack on the ground and walked over to join Meredith near the heater. "I couldn't find you at first, but then I heard you working in here. Where's Duke?"

"He saw a rabbit, and I let him out to investigate." Meredith set down the stack of empty plastic trays next to her growing media. Even if her reason for expanding the business wanted nothing to do with her, Marcus would still want his microgreens.

"You can use this greenhouse too now?"

"The repair guys finished up about noon." Meredith rubbed her arms together. With the heater running all the time, the greenhouse would eventually warm up, but it was still nippy in here. She'd start this row of trays, get back inside the house where it was warm, and offer Hailey some herbal tea.

Even if Ava was mad at her, even if she never moved back to Abundance, Meredith still had Zach in her life. And Hailey, who—unlike Ava—still wanted to be around her.

Every afternoon this week, except yesterday when she had her Wednesday play practice, Hailey had stopped by after she got off the bus. "One of these days, I'm going to convince Dad we need both a horse and a dog," she'd said on Monday. "In the meantime, you don't mind if I come by to pet Duke and talk with you, do you?"

"Are you kidding? Duke likes you even better than Milk Bones, and I love getting the chance to hear about your day." Meredith had checked with Zach about Hailey stopping by when he called Monday night. Once she'd assured him that the girl was no bother, that she was happy to have the company, he'd been thrilled.

"If she hangs out with you," he said, "it's way safer than what she wanted to do last week—ride the bus home from school every day with Kayla so the two of them could double up and ride Kayla's horse together, unsupervised."

Meredith wasn't a parent, but she had to agree. The greenhouse was definitely safer. Besides, she enjoyed seeing Hailey when she first came home, being there while she decompressed after school.

Maybe she wasn't really up to enjoying anything today, but...

She tried to force thoughts of Ava out of her mind and, although her head was beginning to hurt, dredged up a smile. "How was your day at middle school?"

Duke barked outside the door of the greenhouse, apparently more interested in seeing his new best friend than in chasing rabbits.

Hailey dashed back to the door to let him in, then patted his back and told him how much she loved him. "School wasn't too bad," she said to Meredith. "I got an *A* on my English paper, and I sat with the other Hailey again at lunch."

"Hailey Zimmerman? I know her mom. She's really nice."

"So is Hailey Z." She and Duke walked closer to

Meredith. "Pretty much everybody's been nice here. It's totally different from my school in Arizona. I'm so glad we moved."

Duke whined, trotted back toward the door of the greenhouse, and barked.

"You were just out, boy. I'm sure that rabbit is long gone." Meredith pressed a hand against the side of her head. The headache she'd been trying to ignore was getting worse. Most likely, it was tension from her fight with Ava. "What was your English paper on, Hailey?"

"'The Raven,' by Edgar Allan Poe." Hailey described the process they'd used in writing the paper, something about rough drafts and reading a classmate's paper and making helpful suggestions and how she was beginning to like Mrs. Dawson and...

Meredith stopped working, set down her tools, and rubbed both temples. Her head hurt so much that it was getting hard to focus. She was almost dizzy.

"Meredith?" Hailey's voice sounded wobbly. "I feel weird." She limply petted Duke, who was back beside them, still whining. Then she sat down and leaned against the leg of one of the tables.

Meredith's pulse sped. "Hailey, what's wrong?"

"I'm so sleepy," Hailey mumbled.

What was going on? If Hailey was feeling odd and her own head was killing her and Duke was acting weird and—

Oh my word—the heater!

"Hailey, come on. We have to get out of here." She tried to get Hailey to stand, and when that didn't work, she grabbed the girl under the arms and pulled her toward the door. Despite the fact that Hailey couldn't weigh more than a hundred pounds, Meredith felt as if she was fighting her way through syrup. She could barely move her.

And, like the tide easing into a protected bay, a fog seemed to fall over her mind. Nothing in the world had ever seemed as appealing as lying down on the soft, comfortable gravel floor of the greenhouse.

No! Meredith shook her head vigorously. She stumbled to the door, opened it, and drew in a deep breath of fresh air. "Wake up," she yelled at herself. "You can't let anything happen to Hailey."

Then she raced back, gripped Hailey under the arms again, and tugged.

She managed to move her at least ten inches.

Again and again, she grabbed Hailey under her arms and pulled.

Bit by bit, though the progress seemed to grow slower, Meredith moved Hailey closer to the door.

At last she pulled her outside. She drew in a clean, crisp lungful of air and dragged the girl out onto the grass. "Hailey," she shouted.

Hailey didn't reply, and Duke was still inside the greenhouse, lying on the ground.

Meredith's heart felt like it was ripping apart. *Please, God, please let them be okay.* "Hailey!"

The girl's eyelids fluttered. "What's wrong with me?"

"The heater must have leaked carbon monoxide." Meredith pulled off her jacket and pillowed it under Hailey's head. "Stay here and take deep breaths. I'm going back in for Duke."

"Duke!" Hailey tried to raise herself up.

"No," Meredith shouted. "Stay here. Do you have your phone?"

Hailey pawed the ground around her, as if her phone might be there, then blinked and pulled it from her pocket. "I've got it."

"Call 911." Meredith held Hailey's shoulder and looked her squarely in the eye. "Even if I don't come out"—she searched her fuzzy mind for some reason that would keep Hailey outside—"you need to be here to tell the paramedics where I am. Promise me that no matter what, you will not go back in the greenhouse."

"Okay. I promise." Hailey's voice came out shaky and she sank back down, but she dialed quickly.

Thank goodness. Hopefully the ambulance would be here soon, and Hailey would be okay. But Duke was still inside. Meredith rushed back toward the greenhouse.

"Prop the door open," Hailey called.

Oh, yeah. Good idea. Meredith wedged a piece of mulch from the flowerbed under the edge of the door to keep it open. Then she took a deep gasp of clean air, held her breath, and went back inside.

But she only took a few steps before the carbon monoxide she'd already breathed took its toll. She couldn't hold her breath any longer. She had to inhale.

Things began to get blurry.

The white pieces of gravel looked like little pillows.

What was she here for?

What was...?

Chapter Twelve

Zach positioned the white cardboard box in the exact center of the front passenger seat of his SUV and promised himself that he'd take every corner slowly as he drove home. After all, a whole pecan pie from Cassidy's Diner was important cargo, well worth the stop after he left Stacey's office.

His shirt pocket held something even more valuable, a flash drive Stacey had given him with hundreds of photos of the Abundance area. While they talked, she'd also emailed him statistics that would add even more information to the prospectus for the solar project, letting investors see what a benefit it would be for the community.

Sure, the fact that Joe Webster was no longer on board was a huge concern. But Zach would simply have to find new backers, maybe even some from Abundance or the surrounding area. People liked investing in ventures that helped the local economy, and the solar farm should create at least ten full-time permanent jobs. Not as big an impact as a manufacturing plant coming in, but enough to make a difference in a town as small as Abundance. One way or another, he was determined to make this project work. He and Cliff would find a way to get the money they needed. They'd done it before. They could do it again.

Obstacles cropped up, but with hard work and the right attitude, he could overcome them. He simply needed to focus on the positives, like the fact that when he'd stopped at Cassidy's for pie, they happened to have Hailey's favorite flavor, pecan, on the menu.

He couldn't wait to taste it. The sweet scent of the rich filling and the buttery pastry filled every inch of his SUV. No matter how much dinner he ate, he wanted a large slice of pie for dessert. Was a quarter of the pie too large of a serving to eat at one sitting or—?

His phone rang and Hailey's number appeared on the dashboard screen.

He tapped a button on the steering wheel to connect the call. "Hi, sweetie. I'm bringing home a surprise!" She was going to love the pie. He'd even ask if she wanted to invite Meredith to come over after supper to join them.

"Dad…" Hailey sounded woozy. "I need…help."

His muscles tensed. "What's wrong? Where are you?"

"At Meredith's greenhouse. We got carbon dioxide poisoning from the heater."

Carbon dioxide poisoning?

No. A chill ran through him. She meant carbon *mon*oxide, which if the concentration was high enough, could kill a person in less than an hour. His pulse began to pound. "Hailey, listen to me. You need to get outside."

"I…am."

Thank God. "Did you call 911?"

"I did, and they're coming. They told me to stay on the line, but I dropped the phone and it hung up, and I didn't know if I should call them back. And Meredith's still inside, trying to get Duke out."

"She's still inside the greenhouse?"

"Yes, and she said I had to stay outside to watch for the ambulance to tell the paramedics where she was. She made me promise not to go back in, no matter what."

Zach's skin grew clammy as he understood what Meredith hadn't told Hailey, understood what "no matter what" meant. "She's, uh, she's right, Hailey. You *have* to stay outside."

"Okay. I will." Hailey cut out for a moment, then came back on the line, sounding stronger. "Dad, 911 is calling me back."

"Answer it, and I'll be there soon. Make sure you tell them to go to Lawson's Organic Farms on County Road 1400. Tell them to look for the greenhouses." He hung up.

A few minutes later he screeched around the corner onto the county road, trying to reassure himself.

Hailey is outside. Meredith is strong. They'll be all right. They'll be fi—

The back of his throat burned, and he pounded a fist on the steering wheel. It was no use telling himself things that might be lies.

He had no idea how high of a level of carbon monoxide Hailey had been exposed to or how long the exposure had been. The smaller a person, the worse the effects, right? Hailey was only thirteen and so slender. He'd brought her to Abundance to make her life better, but what if moving here had been a horrible mistake?

And Meredith, sweet Meredith, who even in a crisis had protected his girl by making her promise not to go back in the greenhouse, was still in grave danger. What if the exposure had already been too much for her?

Without warning, memories flooded his mind. Of the hospital in Phoenix, of the doctor coming out to tell him that both Jillian and the baby had died, of the day his heart had been ripped in two.

He drew in a ragged breath and gripped the steering wheel so tightly that his knuckles turned white.

Even at the speed he was driving, he was at least five minutes away where there was nothing, nothing he could do to help.

But...

An unspoken prayer welled up inside him, a plea for God to protect Hailey and Meredith.

Five minutes later, Zach whipped his SUV off the county road and onto the gravel drive to the left of Meredith's house, the one that led around back to the greenhouses.

The greenhouse that had been damaged was now covered with shiny new plastic.

He drove around the corner of the house and spotted Hailey in the grass, leaning against the base of a tree.

But he didn't see an ambulance or Meredith.

Heart pounding, he parked, leapt out of his car, and raced toward Hailey, then bent down to check on her. "Are you okay? Is Meredith—"

"My head hurts, but I think I'm okay."

His muscles suddenly went weak, and his breath whooshed out as he pulled her into a tight hug. She sounded steadier than she had on the phone, and her eyes had focused sharply on him.

"Meredith still hasn't come out." Hailey pointed to the repaired greenhouse.

His stomach knotted.

The door was propped open. But how long had Meredith been in there and how close was she to the source of the carbon monoxide?

"I'm going in for her. You do your best to flag down the ambulance when you see it." He hated to leave Hailey, but he sprinted toward the greenhouse and—right before he went inside—drew in a deep breath of fresh air.

A few feet inside, his heart clenched.

Halfway back from the door, Meredith lay on the ground, slumped together with Duke. She lay motionless, face flushed. Was he too late? Was she already—?

He bent closer and saw her fingers flutter.

Thank you, God. Thank you. Emotion welled inside him, but he pushed it down. He didn't have time to waste. Quickly, he picked her up and carried her toward the door, fighting the need to breathe with every step.

Finally, lungs burning, he burst outside and lowered her to the ground. He gasped for air, then managed to speak. "Meredith? Can you hear me?"

She drooped in his arms, limp and unresponsive.

His heart plummeted. He'd hoped the fresh air was all she needed. He didn't know what else to do, and the ambulance still hadn't arrived.

"Is she okay?" Hailey asked. And into the phone she

said, "My dad just brought her out, but she's not moving."

"She has a pulse." Zach moved Meredith to a spot where the grass looked softer and laid her down. He held a hand under her nose until he felt her breath lightly flow against his skin. "And she's breathing." He stood and scanned the horizon, straining his ears for the faintest change in sound.

Nothing.

Then, far in the distance, came the siren's wail.

He ran toward the road, waving his arms.

The ambulance came into view and slowed once the driver spotted him.

Zach pointed to the drive to the greenhouse and sprinted across the yard to Meredith and Hailey. "Over here!" he shouted. "We need help!"

Two men climbed out and raced over, edging him out of the way as he explained that he thought they had carbon monoxide poisoning. One paramedic checked Hailey's vitals, while the other put an oxygen mask on Meredith.

Zach looked from Hailey to Meredith and back again. There wasn't anything more he could for them, but maybe he could still help Duke. "There's a dog inside," he called to the paramedics. "It may be too late, but I've got to try. I'll hold my breath the entire time."

"Sir, no! Don't go in," one of the paramedics shouted.

Zach ignored him, took another deep breath, and ran inside the greenhouse.

Duke had vomited and now lay on the ground, weak.

Zach gently scooped him up and, as quickly as possible, got him outside. He placed him on the grass a few feet away from Hailey, Meredith, and the paramedics.

One of the paramedics turned to him, his face lined with concern. "Did you breathe any of the fumes in there?"

"No, not at all. I'm fine, but Duke…" He gestured to the dog, who, though conscious, still looked weak.

"We have to get the human patients stabilized first." The paramedic returned to caring for Hailey.

Zach nodded.

If only the ambulance had come with a third paramedic, one to help Duke. Zach gently rubbed the dog's head. "Hang in there, big fella."

Wait—

Hailey had said a vet had a practice at her home nearby. When they were at Whole Hog, Meredith had mentioned the woman's name. What was it? Cartwright? No. That wasn't it.

Zach pulled his phone from his pocket and called his dad, who knew the vet and quickly found the number.

Cathy Wainwright answered on the first ring, said she had just closed the office for the day, and promised to be at the greenhouses in two minutes.

True to her word, while the paramedics were still working with Hailey and Meredith, she pulled in the driveway. He helped her load Duke in her car, and she said she would start him on oxygen immediately.

One of the paramedics, the one who'd told Zach not to go in the greenhouse, called out his thanks to the vet as she pulled away, then he jogged over to Zach. "Sir, we've got them both stabilized, and we're ready to leave. I want to check you out first, though."

Zach protested but quickly realized it was faster to agree. Soon he was given the all clear, and a few minutes later, he was back on County Road 1400, driving behind the ambulance, its siren blaring.

He hugged the larger vehicle's back bumper but got stopped at a red light near the hospital. No matter how much he wanted to be with Hailey and Meredith, he shouldn't cause someone else to have a wreck.

So he waited, drumming his fingers on the steering wheel, at the light. After a few seconds, he glanced down and spotted something white on the floorboards of the passenger side. The box that held the pecan pie, tipped on its side.

A bittersweet ache rushed through his chest. Before, it had seemed so important to get that pie home safely.

Now he couldn't care less.

All he wanted was for Hailey to be fine.

And for Meredith to open her eyes.

Once at the hospital, Zach parked as close as he could without being in a tow-away zone and scrambled out of his SUV. He dashed up to the ambulance just as the paramedics brought Hailey out on a gurney. Her nose and mouth were covered by a mask, and her eyes were wide and frightened.

Zach moved to her side. "I'm here, sweetie."

The tension around her eyes eased, and she reached toward his hand.

He slipped his fingers into hers, and she squeezed them tightly, making the back of his throat grow raw. *Thank you, thank you, thank you, God.* She was awake. She was alert. She was at the hospital where they could take care of her.

But Meredith was nowhere to be seen.

He looked over at one of the paramedics. "Where's the other patient, the woman?"

"On her way to treatment." He moved Hailey's hand back inside the rails of the gurney. "Sir, we need you to go to the desk and fill out the paperwork." He pushed the gurney toward the open double doors, where a woman in scrubs waited.

"I'll be with you soon, Hailey," Zach said.

Inside, he sped to the admissions desk for the ER. He stood in line, alternating between peering over the shoulder of the woman ahead of him and reading about carbon monoxide poisoning on his phone.

Halfway down a web page, a paragraph caught his eye. "Depending on the amount of exposure, carbon monoxide can cause permanent damage to a child's heart or brain. Severe exposure can cause neurological symptoms weeks later."

His chest tightened as he stared at his phone. Permanent damage. Oh, his poor Hailey.

He tapped his foot and inched forward, crowding the woman in front of him, who was still talking to the clerk at the desk.

After what seemed like hours, the woman shot an annoyed look over her shoulder at him and moved away.

He lurched forward. "Zach Gilcroft. My daughter was brought in with carbon monoxide poisoning. Can you tell me anything about her condition or anything about the woman she came in with, Meredith Lawson?"

The receptionist picked up the reading glasses that hung on a chain around her neck, perched them on her nose, and punched a few keys on the computer. "I don't have any answers for you, sir. I need to get some information and then you can go back and ask the nurse." She began asking questions.

In a normal situation, Zach would have said the receptionist was efficient. After what he'd read on the internet, the intake process seemed interminable.

Finally, though, the receptionist handed back his insurance card. "Your daughter is in Room 6. Just go through that door and—"

He didn't stick around to hear the rest. If the rooms were numbered, he'd find Room 6.

Less than a minute later, he did.

"Hailey?" He pushed the curtain back.

"Dad!" She sat up on the gurney and pulled the mask off her mouth and nose.

Warmth surged through his chest. "Oh, sweetie!" He rushed in, pulled her into his arms, and squeezed her tight.

"Put that mask back on, young lady." A stern voice rang out behind him.

Zach turned.

A dark-haired nurse watched until Hailey complied, then turned to Zach. "You're her father?"

He stepped toward her. "Zach Gilcroft. Is she okay?"

"She should be, but she needs to get more oxygen into her system as quickly as she can."

"Should she go to a hospital in Columbia or Kansas City?" He lowered his voice, hoping that Hailey wouldn't hear. "Are her heart and brain okay? Are you worried about neurological damage that may show up later?"

"If Dr. Brannon had any concerns, he would have already transferred her." She moved to Hailey's side and checked her monitors, making notes on a laptop in a businesslike fashion. As if it was all routine. As if Hailey was one more patient in an assembly line.

"Are you sure she's okay?" Zach couldn't keep the note of worry out of his tone.

The nurse looked up at him. Her face softened, her briskness fell away, and she spoke gently. "Dad, your girl is going to be fine. Her numbers are almost back to normal already."

Zach's eyes prickled. "Thank you." *Fine.* His girl was going to be fine. He wasn't going to lose her.

God was so good.

He gripped Hailey's hand, careful not to interfere with the oxygen tube, and turned to the nurse. "Can you tell me anything about the woman who came in with Hailey, Meredith Lawson?"

"I'm afraid I can't discuss another patient." The brisk tone was back. "Confidentiality," she said as she left.

He should have expected that. As soon as he spent a few more minutes with Hailey, he'd go to the nurse's station and ask. Perhaps if he found a different nurse, one who was nice all the time, not just sometimes, he'd be able to find out how Meredith was.

For now, he sank into a chair, shaky from adrenaline, and squeezed Hailey's hand. "I'm so glad you're okay."

"Eeee Ooo," Hailey said through the mask.

Her words were muffled, but Zach was pretty sure she'd said, "Me too."

A few moments later, his phone dinged, and she jerked her head up.

He pulled the phone from his pocket and read the text.

"It's the vet. She can't guarantee it, but she thinks Duke will be okay."

Hailey's eyes shone, and she raised a fist in victory.

Another blessing.

Hailey was fine. Duke was doing better.

But what about Meredith?

Chapter Thirteen

Meredith pulled up the extra blanket the nurse had given her, tucked it around her shoulders, and looked at the hospital room where she'd be spending the night. After she'd arrived at the hospital in Abundance, because she'd been exposed to carbon monoxide longer than Hailey, she'd been transferred to a different ambulance and driven to one of the big hospitals in Columbia because she needed special treatment to get oxygen into her blood even faster.

Now, finally alone, all that had happened came rushing back, and she tried not to cry.

How could she have been so careless?

The minute she got that headache, she should have realized something was wrong and made Hailey leave the greenhouse. Had she done that?

No.

The past couple of years, ever since that big windstorm, when the HVAC guys came out to do their annual check, she'd told them not to worry about the broken greenhouse. When she'd had the plastic repaired—was it only this morning?—she should have requested they come back before she started it up.

Had she done that?

No. The HVAC check was something she did every September. When it came up on her calendar, she scheduled it. Even though putting the repaired greenhouse back in operation should have reminded her to call them, it hadn't. Instead, because she was so upset after talking with Ava, she hadn't even thought of it.

Wasn't it enough that fourteen years ago she'd caused the death of both her parents by thinking only of herself? That she'd made Ava feel like a burden ever since?

Apparently not. Today she'd put Hailey in danger.

Tears welled in her eyes.

Meredith blinked furiously, but the tears escaped and ran down her cheeks, soaking the pillowcase.

Her fault.

Her fault.

All her fault.

But now that the doctors and nurses had left her alone, now that her no-phone-allowed treatment session was over, she could at least check on Hailey.

She swallowed hard, grabbed her phone, and typed out a text to Zach. *How is Hailey?*

A few seconds later, he replied. *She's fine. The nurse says her levels are almost back to normal.*

Meredith's chest wrenched and the tears that had only leaked out before now poured down her cheeks. She wasn't sure she would have been able to stand it if Hailey had been injured. She let out a shaky sigh and blew her nose.

Little dots appeared on her screen. Zach was typing again.

After a moment, his text came through.

They won't tell me how you're doing. Are you okay?

Physically? Yeah. The doctor said she might be tired and have headaches for several weeks, but he didn't see signs of permanent damage. He said she'd been lucky. If she'd been in the greenhouse any longer or if she had any underlying health conditions, she might have had serious complications. All of that was more than Zach needed to know, so she simply typed, *I'm okay. I'm so glad Hailey is well. I'm very, very sorry about what happened.*

Zach's next message appeared almost instantly.

Are you still in the ER? Can I come see you?

He thought she was still back at the hospital in Abundance, and he wanted to see her.

An ache built in her chest as she realized what she needed to do.

Didn't he understand what a danger she was to him and Hailey? Her very presence put loved ones around her at risk. Didn't he realize that all she should be was their neighbor? Not even a close neighbor. Not someone they did things with. Just someone who lived next door that waved in passing. Nothing more.

She forced herself to type out another message.

I'm not really ready for visitors. Give me a minute and I'll call you.

Then she took a sip of water from the giant plastic cup the nurse had set on her bedside table, raised the head of the bed, and steeled herself.

There was no use putting it off. It would be more polite to tell him in person, but the sooner she ended things, the better.

Hailey pulled the oxygen mask away from her face. "Are you sure she's okay?"

Zach frowned and covered his own nose and mouth with his hand until she replaced her mask. "That's better."

She waved her hands in frustration.

Oh, he hadn't answered her question. "Meredith says she's okay. I'll ask more when she calls, but I think if something was wrong, she'd tell me."

Partly muffled by the mask, Hailey said, "I don't want anything to happen to her."

"She's really special, isn't she?"

Hailey nodded dramatically and crossed her hands over her heart.

Zach patted her shoulder and spoke softly. "I'll take the call out in the hall, so I don't disturb the people on the other side of the curtain, but you text me if the nurse or the doctor comes in."

Hailey gave a thumb's up just as his phone rang with an incoming video call.

He answered it halfway through the first ring. "Meredith?" His voice quavered, the stress of the day breaking through.

"Hi, Zach."

"Hey. I'm just stepping out of the ER to talk with you." He waved to Hailey and slipped into the hall, where he gazed into the phone and let out a shaky breath. "Are you really alright?"

"I am." She sounded exhausted. Her hair hung limp. And her eyes were red, underlined with dark circles, and filled with misery.

Even so, seeing those eyes open was literally an answered prayer. All the while, as he'd carried her out of the greenhouse, waited off to the side while the paramedics took care of her, and sat with Hailey in the ER, he'd been worried about Meredith, afraid he might never see her beautiful brown eyes again.

Her chin trembled. "When you go back in the ER, can you tell Hailey I'm sorry?"

"I will, but really, she's okay. Eager to be released and begging to drive through The Burger Hut on the way home so she can get a cheeseburger."

Meredith's mouth twisted as if even the idea of one of their greasy burgers made her a little nauseous.

"Not what you'd want to eat after carbon monoxide poisoning?"

"No way." She shuddered.

"Me neither, but I guess if she wants to eat their food, she's fully recovered, and I really don't need to worry about neurological damage showing up later."

Meredith's face tightened.

"I read too much on the internet. The doctor assured me that she's healthy."

"I understand why you were worried," Meredith said quietly. "Hailey means the world to you. I'm very glad she's recovering."

"I'm glad you are too."

Meredith looked away.

Unease needled his stomach. "What's going on?"

Her jaw stiffened, her throat moved up and down as she swallowed, and for a long moment she didn't say anything. "I...I don't think we should go out anymore."

His chest went numb. Not go out? He wandered into the waiting area for lab tests and sank into a chair. "Why not?"

A sheen of tears glistened in her eyes. "Because I nearly killed your daughter."

"Meredith." Just like with her parents' death, she was taking too much of the responsibility on herself. "It wasn't your fault. I assume the heat exchanger cracked. Sometimes, even when they're new, they fail."

"It *was* my fault." Her face twisted in anguish. "The heater was far from new, and I hadn't had it checked in years. I know better. I know carbon monoxide can be a danger in a greenhouse, but I was so eager to get more microgreens planted that I didn't think."

His stomach sank, and a chill radiated out from his core. "You were running equipment without doing any safety checks? You're lucky you and Hailey weren't both killed."

Meredith's face crumpled. "I know. It was totally irresponsible."

He opened his mouth to agree, then clamped it shut and stared at her face on the screen, unable to accept what she'd done.

He'd been terrified that he would lose her. That he would lose Hailey. That it was Jillian and the baby all over again and he'd lose both of them. All because Meredith had been using an old, broken-down heater that she hadn't examined in years.

With no safety precautions at all?

If he'd let Hailey go riding with Kayla, she might have suffered from a serious fall. Instead, believing it would be safer, he'd let her spend time with Meredith.

Where she might have died.

Thank goodness his girl had the good sense to get out of that greenhouse when she did.

He'd thought things in Abundance were so wonderful. He'd even thought he and Meredith had a future together. Thought he'd found a woman he could trust.

But what kind of future could they have if he couldn't trust her with the most important thing of all? With Hailey?

None. Absolutely none.

His heart twisted, and he slumped in the waiting room chair. "I'm sorry, but I guess you're right." He couldn't date someone who'd put Hailey at risk. After what he'd been through, he simply couldn't. "We shouldn't see each other anymore." He jabbed at the button to end the call.

Chapter Fourteen

After breakfast, Zach stared out his kitchen window at the rain pouring down on the site for the solar panels. Even if the panels had already been installed, today was no day for generating megawatt hours.

The storm had started late, after he and Hailey returned from the hospital, and after some initial thunder and lightning, it had eased to a quiet, steady downpour.

He'd already phoned the school, told them what happened, and explained that he was letting his daughter sleep in and keeping her home today to rest. If he also wanted her home so he could hug her a few dozen times to reassure himself she was safe, that was his business.

Yesterday had been one of the longest days of his life. He'd been so frightened that Hailey or Meredith would die.

Then he'd had that awful realization that no matter how much he wanted to, he couldn't trust Meredith. The optimism he'd had for their relationship evaporated, replaced by the same feeling he'd had after Jillian died. That his lungs had been filled with steel wool. That the tendons in his shoulders had been replaced with steel bars. That he and he alone had to protect his girl from a million enemies, seen and unseen, who were ready to attack at any time. That there was no one he could turn to. No one he could trust.

And he probably could have handled things better with Meredith.

In the end, though, it would have turned out the same. He shouldn't be in a relationship with anyone. He had his daughter, he had his work, and he had his dad, and Stacey, and her son George, as well as his sister who lived out of town. That should be enough for anyone. It would be. It—

A car rumbled into his driveway.

He walked toward the front of the house to look out to see who it was, but before he got to the living room, the back door banged open.

"Zach?"

He raced toward the kitchen. "Stacey, keep your voice down. Hailey's still asleep. She was injured yesterday, and we were at the ER until nearly midni—"

"I know all about that." His sister stood in the middle of his kitchen, brown hair bunched up in some clip thing, dark eyes blazing. "I can't believe I had to hear about it from other people. Louise Wilkers and then two other calls, one right after another, and neither of them was from you."

"I was going to call later this morning. I..." He scratched his cheek. "Hold on. How do you know what happened? Isn't everyone at the hospital bound by patient confidentiality?"

"The people who work there are. The other patients *aren't,* and people can hear everything that goes on in that ER through those little curtains. Now, first of all"—her tone grew gentler—"is Hailey really all right?"

"She is. The doctor assured me she'll be fine. He said she must have gotten out of the greenhouse pretty quickly."

"Good." Stacey planted her hands on her hips. "Then I don't need to worry about her. I need to worry about you, my moron brother."

"I am not a moron."

"If not, you're the rudest man I've ever met. If Hailey's alright, why didn't you go get Meredith down in Columbia this morning?"

A brick lodged sideways in Zach's throat. "Columbia?"

"You didn't know? Louise said Meredith called her early this morning and asked her to drive down and pick her up. Apparently the local hospital doesn't have the treatment Meredith needed, and she had to spend the night in Columbia. Did you just drive home last night and forget all about her getting home?"

His shoulders sank. "Well, yeah, I guess I did." He edged back until his hips rested against the kitchen counter. "I didn't even know she'd been taken to Columbia." On the phone she'd said she was fine, but clearly she'd been in more danger than Hailey. "But we'd broken up."

"Why on earth would you two break up? I don't know her well, but Meredith seems like exactly what you need in your life. Really, she might even be a better fit for you than my friend that I wanted to set you up with."

"Not that it's any of your business, but I can't trust

Meredith with Hailey. The whole carbon monoxide thing happened because she didn't have the HVAC system inspected. She was asking for an accident to happen, all because she was in a hurry to get more plants started."

Stacey's eyebrows shot up. "So she made a mistake because she rushed into something. I realize you don't want Hailey endangered, but you're the last person in the world who has any room to complain. Haven't we had several conversations on the phone where you mentioned jumping into some venture and needing your partner to clean up all the details?"

"Those were business deals not safety risks."

Stacey leaned in closer. "And didn't you tell me how proud you were of Meredith that she was getting that greenhouse repaired?"

"Well, yeah, but I expected her to do things properly." He did not need a lecture from his older sister. He walked to the back door, ready to open it and encourage her to head on home.

"If you knew about the repairs, why didn't *you* mention that she should do safety checks?"

His hand froze on the doorknob.

"Well, why didn't you?"

The brick that had been lodged in his throat now landed in his stomach.

She was right. His annoying older sister was right. There was no reason why he couldn't have reminded Meredith to think about safety. He'd been the one encouraging her, and was possibly part of the reason she moved so fast with her expansion. He'd even been the one who pushed things with Marcus so she'd earn more from her produce, getting her even more fired up about the potential for extra profit.

Yet what had he done last night? He'd placed all the blame on her, ignoring his own possible role. Then he'd left her to find her own way home after she'd been taken to a hospital an hour away.

His stomach started to churn, and he felt hot and cold at the same time.

How could he have done that to Meredith? How could he have made her feel worse about what happened? Meredith, the woman who was still miserable, years later, from guilt over her parents' death?

"Everyone makes mistakes, Zach," Stacey said, still in lecture mode. "We have to forgive them."

He nodded stiffly. She was right. Again. Meredith had never meant to hurt Hailey. Forgiving her was the decent thing to do. The importance of forgiveness was even in the Bible, more than once. And forgiving her was definitely the right thing to do when he could be partly to blame himself. He couldn't expect her to be perfect when he wasn't perfect himself.

"I need to see her." He pulled out his phone and sent her a text, asking if he could stop by. "I've got to apologize. I never should have acted like it was Meredith's fault that Hailey nearly died."

"You blamed Meredith?" Hailey stood in the doorway from the hall.

"Sweetie, I didn't realize you were up."

"It's kind of hard to sleep with you and Aunt Stacey yelling at each other." She took a step toward the kitchen, then stopped, gasped, and cupped her hand over her mouth, then let it fall. "Dad, didn't I tell you? Meredith's not the reason I almost died. She's the reason I'm alive."

"What?" Zach said, the word coming out in unison with Stacey.

"Meredith saved me." Hailey walked closer, face earnest. "I got so sleepy. I wouldn't have gotten outside if she hadn't helped me. She basically carried me out."

The queasy, churning feeling in Zach's stomach was gone. Completely gone. Replaced by a numbness that started in his gut and flowed outward. "I...I...I've got to get ready." He headed up the stairs.

And he managed to keep it together until he saw the photos in the hall. Until he saw Jillian's face.

Pain hit his chest like a spear, and he stumbled toward the shower, where he let the tears flow.

Aw, Jillian, I need to forgive you too.

I don't know why you wanted another baby so much, but deep down I know you loved Hailey and I know you loved me. Maybe because you were so young, you really didn't believe you could die. Maybe you just had some need, deep inside, for another child that had nothing to do with me. Whatever the reason, if there is anything there to blame, I forgive you. I forgive you completely. And I'm sorry I was so angry with you, and sorry I shoved my emotions down for so long. That only made it harder to heal.

You were a good mom. And a good wife.

Zach let out a ragged breath.

Then he stood under the spray, letting the water pour over his face.

He couldn't bring Jillian back. He couldn't undo the past six years of holding onto his pain.

But he could move forward.

Starting with prayer.

❦

"I'm here to pick up Duke." Meredith pushed back the hood of her raincoat and set her keys and Duke's leash on the counter at Cathy Wainwright's veterinary clinic. Normally, with Cathy's clinic so close, she would have walked, but five minutes ago it had been pouring. No need to get Duke soaking wet if he wasn't feeling well.

"Oh, I'm so glad he's better. He's such a nice dog," the receptionist said. "Let me tell Dr. Cathy you're here. Please, have a seat. It may be a few minutes before Duke's ready." She disappeared down a hallway.

Last night, Meredith had found a message on her phone from the vet. Cathy, who must have been called by the paramedics, said Duke would only need to spend one night in the clinic and could come home after breakfast. As soon as Meredith got back in town, she'd come over to get him.

From somewhere in the back of the clinic, a dog barked, but it was a high-pitched yip. Not Duke.

Meredith told herself to be patient and looked around the office. The dog side of the clinic was empty, except for her. One wall was mostly windows, while another displayed a poster showing different breeds of dogs. On the other side of the half wall that divided the dog side of the office from the cat side, an older couple sat with a pet carrier, and a plump, fluffy orange cat lounged on the counter. Jack O. Lantern, one of the friendliest cats Meredith had ever met, not only starred in every ad Cathy Wainwright ran in the paper, but he also had his run of the office. Or at least the cat portion of it.

Meredith leaned her head to one side, trying to catch a glimpse of Duke coming down the hall. No sign of him yet. Soon, though, she'd be able to see him. Even though Cathy said in her phone message that Duke would be okay, Meredith had been worried. Plus, she'd missed him so much. She'd only gone inside for a few moments after Louise dropped her off, but her house had seemed empty without him.

She'd felt so alone. No Duke. No Ava. No Hailey.

No Zach.

This morning at the hospital, when she got back to her room after a final test, she'd found three texts from him.

That had been the last thing she needed, more accusation and anger. She hit Delete without reading them, then sat on her rumpled bed and cried.

This breakup was horrible, but it was the best thing to do for Zach and Hailey. Maybe even for her as well. What if she and Zach had dated for weeks or even months before he figured out that she wasn't suitable to be a mom to Hailey? That he could do better?

The longer the two of them were together before things ended, the more painful it would be.

She simply had to be strong and move on, one day at a time. Having Duke home to keep her company would help.

Her phone rang, and she pulled it from her pocket.

Ava. Probably also still mad at her. Meredith couldn't deal with that now.

She shut the phone off and sent a quick text, telling Ava that she was busy and would call her back.

Two seconds later, Ava called again.

Meredith picked up and spoke quietly, trying not to disturb the people sitting on the cat side of the lobby. "I'm in the vet's office, waiting to get Duke. I'll call you back in ten minutes."

"Wait!" Ava cried. "Did you really have carbon monoxide poisoning?" She didn't sound angry, only concerned.

"Yeah." Meredith went to the corner of the lobby farthest from the half-wall divider, sat in a wooden chair, and twisted her body to face the outside wall. She didn't want the details of her trip to the ER shared with the whole town.

"Are you okay?"

"I'm fine, but how did you hear about it?"

"Zach called me."

"Zach? Why—?"

"He's trying to find you and somehow managed to get my number. He really wants to talk with you and said you aren't answering his texts. What's going on?"

Emotion rose in Meredith's throat. She swallowed back a lump of pain and, as quietly as possible, whispered into the phone. "Things between us aren't going to work out."

"Oh, Meredith, what happened?"

As succinctly as possible, Meredith explained about how she'd neglected to get the HVAC system checked, how she had to be rescued from the greenhouse by the paramedics, and how Hailey had been exposed. "So, you see why Zach needs to find someone else. I almost got his daughter killed."

"Sis, you can't blame yourself. You—"

"Meredith?" Dr. Cathy called from across the room.

"Got to go, Ava. The vet's ready for me." Meredith hung up.

Duke ran toward her, tags jingling, coat gleaming as if he'd just been brushed.

"Oh, Duke!" She knelt down and hugged him with both arms, burying her face in his soft fur. "I'm so glad you're okay." Her throat grew raw, but she forced herself to gain control, then rose and walked to the counter. "Cathy, I can't tell you how much I appreciate what you did."

"No worries," Cathy said. "I'm glad I live close by."

"Me too. Is there anything I need to do to take care of him?"

"Just watch him and try to get him to take it easy for a while."

"Will do." Meredith reached into her purse for her wallet.

Cathy waved a dismissive hand. "No need for that. Our new neighbor Zach called earlier this morning and paid. The one who got Duke out of the greenhouse and phoned me."

Meredith's hand froze halfway out of her purse. Zach was the one who got Duke out of the greenhouse and called Cathy? Not the paramedics? She had no idea he'd even been there. "Um, well, thanks." She snapped the leash onto Duke's collar, still putting the pieces together in her head. She'd assumed Zach met Hailey at the hospital, but maybe when Meredith went back into the greenhouse...

"C'mon, boy. Let's get you home." She walked outside, opened the passenger door of her truck for Duke, and unhooked his leash. He hopped up, ready to go, and tipped his head toward the window, hinting that she should lower it.

"Sorry, buddy, I don't want to let the rain in."

He angled his head toward her, gave her a look that said he loved her anyway, and settled in, tail thumping happily. Even on a wet, gray spring day when he couldn't put his head out the window, Duke loved a good car ride.

Meredith climbed in the truck, and her phone dinged with a text.

Ava again.

You still need to talk to Zach. He must care about you. He tried not to make a big deal of it when we talked on the phone, but it wasn't the paramedics that got you out of that greenhouse. HE did. He basically risked his life to save you.

Meredith's chest went hollow, and she stared at the phone, mouth hanging open.

Chapter Fifteen

Meredith drove straight to Zach's.

The rain had transformed his front yard into a bog, and his gravel driveway had big puddles in it, but she let Duke out of the truck anyway, wanting to keep an eye on him.

After a slow trot to a nearby tree, he returned to her side and stuck by her when she climbed the wide wooden porch steps. It seemed as if he'd missed her as much as she'd missed him.

She patted his head and knocked on the door.

While she waited, she slid back her raincoat hood and brushed a couple of raindrops off her cheeks.

No matter how hard it was, she needed to thank Zach. She'd say a few quick words and go home before she lost her composure.

Inside, she heard footsteps. She looked longingly at her truck, but it was too late to get back in and drive away, and foolish to imagine that only Hailey was home. The footsteps were too heavy to be hers.

The door opened, and Zach stood before her, so handsome it made her heart ache. How was she ever going to talk to him without crying?

"Meredith! Duke! I'm so happy to see you both looking well!" He bent down and rubbed Duke's ears, then straightened and touched Meredith's arm. "I'm glad you're here. I really want to talk with you. I need to tell you—"

She held up a hand. "Wait. I need to say something first."

"Okay. Come on in." He gestured to the living room.

She hesitated. She'd hoped he'd come out on the porch, but he didn't have shoes on. She couldn't very well expect him to walk out into the damp in his socks.

Duke trotted forward, far more eager to go in than she was, but—

She caught hold of his collar and glanced down at his muddy feet.

Zach touched her arm. "Duke too. A little mud is no problem."

Relief rippled through her. "All right, only for a second." Once inside, she stopped in the entryway and squared her shoulders. Best to get this over with. "I want to apologize again for what happened to Hailey. And I'm so sorry that I didn't realize until today that *you* got me out of the greenhouse. I thought it was the paramedics. I don't know how I can ever thank you."

He stepped closer, eyes full of pain. "By forgiving me for how I acted last night on the phone."

"What you said was perfectly justified. What happened to Hailey was all my fault, and it was unforgivable."

"No. What happened was an accident. If anyone *is* to blame, it's not just you, it's me too. I should have suggested a safety review. We do them on all our projects."

She gave him a wry smile. "That's stretching things. The truth of the matter is that I nearly got your daughter killed."

"Meredith." He took her hand and led her to the living room. "Sit." He pointed at the caramel-colored leather couch that faced the fireplace.

She glared at him. "You do realize you're talking to me, not Duke?"

"Frankly"—exasperation rang in his voice—"Duke has more sense."

She pulled her arm away and started toward the door.

He intercepted her, blocking the path, his blue-gray eyes pleading. "No. Please listen to me."

"Fine." Those eyes gave him an unfair advantage, making it impossible for her to say no. She took off her raincoat, crossed the room, and sat at one end of the couch with her coat in her lap, nervously glancing around.

The room looked more like a living room now than it had when they'd gone sledding. The packing boxes were gone. A pile of napkins printed with the name Burger Hut lay on the coffee table, next to a bag of dark chocolate Dove Promises with a couple of pieces spilled out. And a pair of pink socks were wadded up in the other corner of the couch.

Zach tossed the socks on the floor and sat at the other end of the couch, facing her. "Even when we try to stay on top of things, accidents happen. And, even though I didn't know it until this morning, in a moment of crisis in the greenhouse, you saved Hailey's life. You got her out. I can't help but think that God put you there for just that reason."

God? Meredith sniffed. This was ridiculous. "She never would have been there if it hadn't been for me."

"You don't know that. She's been over at your place almost every day. She could easily have wandered into the greenhouse to see how it looked after it was repaired. You don't keep it locked, do you?"

"Well, no," Meredith said slowly, twisting the arm of her raincoat.

Zach leaned closer. "You might have been in town, running errands. I wasn't home. I wouldn't have known she was in danger. She could have died. I didn't think of it at first, but now I think God may have put you there with her so you could rescue her."

Meredith's hands froze while her mind raced, following the logic in what Zach had said. It did sort of make sense. And it did make her feel better. "I hadn't thought of it that way."

"It's not only that." He scooted to the middle of the couch. "For a moment yesterday, I felt I couldn't trust you. But you've shown again and again how much you care about Hailey. That's who you really are." He took her hands in his. "What happened was partly my fault too, but even if you don't accept that, you didn't do it on purpose. And I forgive you."

Emotion pricked the back of Meredith's throat. She did care about Hailey, she really did. And she'd never meant to hurt her.

Zach squeezed her hands. "Meredith, please believe

me. You need to stop blaming yourself for any role you had in the carbon monoxide leak. And in your parents' deaths." He leaned closer. "You forgive other people when they're not perfect, right?"

She twisted her raincoat in her lap. "Well, yeah."

"When they forgive you, you have to accept it. Even if it's a gift you don't feel you deserve, even if you don't feel worthy."

Her heart raced. Heat rushed to her face. And her hands stilled.

Was that her problem all along? That she didn't see her own worth? Was she so busy feeling guilty and beating herself up that she didn't realize that other people valued her more than she valued herself?

Ava had told her again and again that Mom and Dad's deaths weren't her fault, that she didn't blame her at all. Ava had only gotten upset when she thought Meredith wanted to help with the restaurant out of guilt.

Zach was sitting here telling her he'd forgiven her for what had happened to Hailey and that it didn't reflect who she really was. And...

Meredith stared at the candy on the table, the exact same kind as she'd eaten at the bank. A strange mix of weightlessness and incredulity percolated through her. "Dove Promises." She stretched a hand toward the bag.

"They're Hailey's favorite. Do you want one?"

Meredith shook her head numbly. Just seeing them was enough to remind her of what Ellen had said.

That whether or not someone can get a loan doesn't determine the value of their idea. And that the way others treat you doesn't change the value God gave you.

The value God gave you.

Meredith's chest filled with warmth as she suddenly understood. Her breathing eased, and her shoulders, which she hadn't realized were tense, relaxed. Peace flowed through her, new and familiar all at the same time. A peace that felt like coming home.

She'd heard it in church, but she'd managed to distort it and make it somehow less true for her.

That distortion had caused her so much pain.

God loved her, and as his creation, she had worth.

Her value came from him and from how she lived her life, every day. Not just from one or even two mistakes.

And all along, though she'd let her guilt over her parents' deaths stop her from seeing it, he'd loved her. It was if God were a star, shining brightly all the time, and she refused to look up.

How could she not see his love, when she worked each day in the greenhouses, surrounded by the miracle of growth and beauty? How could she not see his love when he'd brought Zach and Hailey into her life?

Today, she simply needed to open her heart to God's love, accept the forgiveness Zach and Ava were offering, and leave her mistakes in the past. Move forward in a relationship with Zach. Move forward being a part of Hailey's life. Even—if Ava was willing—move forward with the restaurant. Most importantly, move forward in a relationship with God that was based in truth, not in lies she told herself.

Maybe today was part of a journey of accepting and understanding how very much God loved her and that he was in control, a journey that would continue, an understanding that would deepen as she continued to grow in her faith.

She slid a trembling hand along the couch toward Zach's. "Oh, thank you. For forgiving me and for helping me finally understand."

He took her hand in his, ran his other hand down her cheek, and cupped her chin. "I love you, Meredith. You're everything I want in my life. For me and for Hailey."

Excitement gushed from her heart like water from a spring, sending tingles down her arms and filling her with a certainty that she and Zach and Hailey were supposed to be together.

"I love you too, Zach," she said softly. "And I love Hailey."

Never in a million years would she have ever dreamed how good it would feel to let go of the guilt she'd carried and let God fully back into her life. Never would she have dreamed she could be so happy. And never would she have dreamed that Zach Gilcroft—so handsome, so smart, so kind and funny—would love her.

She slid her arms around his neck and pulled him closer.

And he leaned down and kissed her.

Zach gave Meredith one last, sweet kiss, and sat back on the couch.

Her cheeks were pink, her brown eyes were shining, and her face seemed lit with happiness.

"You look incredible."

"Thank you." She dipped her head as if embarrassed by the compliment. "I—"

"I saw Meredith's truck." Hailey ran in from the hall. "Is—?" She raced across the room. "Meredith! I'm so glad you're better." She gave Meredith a big hug, then embraced Duke. "And you too." She kissed his head then turned back to Meredith. "You and Dad need to come outside with me to see what's blooming. I spotted them out my window."

Zach raised one eyebrow at Meredith. "What do you think?"

"Sure." She slid on her raincoat. "I don't hear it raining now."

They followed Hailey to the front yard, which seemed even greener than yesterday. Droplets of rain sparkled on the grass and trees, and Hailey stopped beside a wide flowerbed bursting with hundreds of crocuses.

As if on cue, the sun slid from behind a cloud and shone down like a spotlight on the flowerbed, making the bright-yellow and deep-purple blossoms glow.

"See? Aren't they gorgeous?" Hailey waved a hand toward the flowers, looking as proud as if she'd planted them herself.

"They are." Zach stood for a moment, taking in the beauty of God's creation. So much had changed since the day he plowed into Meredith's yard and hit her snowman. When he and Hailey had moved to Abundance, the yard had been so dreary.

Now spring had come to Abundance and to his heart.

He slid an arm around Hailey's shoulders and pulled her to his side. "Hey, I've got a question for you."

She turned to him. Before last night in the ER, he would have been hesitant to ask this in front of Meredith, but now he was sure he knew the answer.

"How would you feel if the two of us spent more time with Meredith? Not just my dating her, but the three of us doing stuff like—" He stopped himself. It was too soon to say *like a family*, even if that was what he wanted. "Like having dinner together once a week?"

Hailey's grin spread wide, and her cheeks rounded. "I'd love it!"

Zach's chest grew warm. They'd start with dinner once a week, then maybe twice. Soon, becoming a family would seem like the most natural thing in the world to all three of them.

But Hailey's eyes narrowed. "Would I still get the horse we talked about this morning?"

Zach groaned. His girl was nothing if not persistent. "Yes. If we can find the right horse." Preferably one that was so old it wouldn't go any faster than a trot. "And if you promise to take care of it."

"I promise." Hailey drew an *X* across her chest.

"What about you?" He pulled Meredith to his other side and looked down into her chocolate-brown eyes. "Would you be interested in more time with Hailey and me?"

"I would." Her eyes met his, shining with love and certainty.

The back of his throat grew scratchy, and he squeezed Meredith and Hailey close, one on either side.

"Hooray!" Hailey slipped away, ran over, and leaned down toward Duke. "Do you hear that, boy? I'm getting everything I've wished for: you and friends and a horse—" She paused, then added with excitement, as if it was by far the most important of all her wishes, "And Meredith!" She ran back and launched herself at Meredith, catching her in a tight hug.

Meredith's eyes shone, and she pulled Hailey close.

Zach stepped back and let out a sigh. When the two of them weren't looking, he brushed aside a tear. What a homecoming. He'd moved back to Abundance hoping his daughter would find friends, and she had, but they'd found so much more.

A second later, Hailey edged over and elbowed Zach.

He glanced down at her. "What?"

"Don't you know anything, Dad?" Hailey rolled her eyes and angled her head toward Meredith. "Now's when you kiss her!"

And he did.

Epilogue

July
Sixteen months later

Meredith sat on a bench outside the old shoe factory a couple of blocks off Main Street and peered into the golden-orange sunset, watching for Zach to return from parking the car. Even now, ten months after they'd gotten married, every time he dropped her off or picked her up at the door when they went out to dinner, she felt treasured.

"Is he coming yet?" Hailey, so grown up at fifteen, sat beside her, wearing a blue sundress that exactly matched her eyes.

"No. He must have had to park all the way in the back. Opening night seems really busy." A flutter of excitement ran through Meredith's chest as she took in the renovated factory.

A vivid green neon sign that read *Ava's* stood out

against the weathered brick, two-story building. Through the windows, Meredith saw diners filling the booths and tables, and every few minutes another couple or family walked toward the door, talking eagerly about the new restaurant.

"Sorry that took so long," Zach said as he came around the corner. "I'd say your sister's got a hit on her hands. The lot is filled. I had to park on a side street." He gently took Meredith's arm and helped her to her feet.

"How are you feeling?" Hailey hovered close beside her.

"Nervous." Meredith had sampled all of Ava's dishes, so she was sure people would like the food, but what if Abundance wasn't big enough to support such an upscale place? What if people wouldn't drive in from out of town after the local novelty wore off? She clasped the strands of her necklace together, unable to contain her jitters. "And, oh, I don't know. This restaurant still doesn't seem real."

"I meant—" Hailey angled her head toward Meredith's mid-section. "How do you feel with the baby? Is coming out tonight too much after you worked all day in the greenhouse?"

"Oh." Meredith ran a hand over her lower back, which had been hurting off and on all day. "I wouldn't want to miss the grand opening." She squeezed Zach's hand. "But I'm okay. I'd say I'm doing about as well as any woman who's sixty-five weeks pregnant."

Hailey giggled.

"It's been eight months and twenty-six days, Meredith." Zach slipped one arm through hers and the other through Hailey's. "Not sixty-five weeks."

178

"Are you sure?" Meredith ran a hand over her belly, which bulged out so far that it looked as if she'd shoved one of those giant exercise balls under her red dress.

"I'm sure."

A silly question. The man kept a calendar with her due date on the refrigerator and had read at least a dozen books about pregnancy.

Once the doctor had told them both that it was safe for her to get pregnant, Zach had been thrilled about the baby.

Until this week, she'd been thrilled too. She'd loved being pregnant. Truly, could anything be more wonderful than being married to Zach, being a mom to Hailey, and knowing that soon there would be another member of their family? And in truth, her pregnancy had been easy. The doctor had been pleased at every checkup, full of reassurance for both her and Zach that all was well. Now, though, it was July in Missouri. The daily highs had been in the 90s and the humidity had been unbearable. This past week, she'd gotten so big that she barely fit between the rows inside the greenhouse. She hadn't even been comfortable last night in the cushy chairs in the church library during the weekly Bible study she and Zach had started attending.

Pregnancy was not all that fun anymore.

Zach guided them toward the door. "Shall we go in?"

They stepped inside and, like with every time she'd been to the restaurant since the renovations were completed, Meredith felt she'd been transported to Kansas City. Or maybe even New York.

Long abandoned, the old shoe factory had been gutted and, with investment from a consortium that Zach had established, completely remodeled inside. The walls were exposed brick, the high ceiling a maze of black pipes. And green plants—including heart-leaf philodendrons and spider plants that Meredith had raised—were tucked in corners, on shelves near the bar, and in wall boxes high above the diners. The scarred hardwood floor had been polished until it gleamed to match the wooden tables, the walls were lined with luxurious brown booths, and brass light fixtures hung over every table, giving each dining space a sense of intimacy.

The hostess welcomed them, then held up a finger and answered her phone headset, explaining that Ava's was booked for the next week. Behind her, almost every chair was filled, and the crowd buzzed with conversation. Even from here, barely into the room, the tantalizing aromas of the menu Ava had been refining and practicing for months swirled around them.

"Meredith!" Ellen from the bank rushed over from a table near the front. "This place is incredible! I can't believe I get to eat in a restaurant this fancy in Abundance!" She touched Meredith's arm. "And I can't ever thank you enough for hiring my nephew Justin. He'd really had a hard time keeping a job before, but he loves working with you."

"He's been such a blessing, Ellen. He does the watering perfectly every time. He's also taken it as his personal duty to check the carbon monoxide detectors every day, which makes both Zach and me happy." Justin, who admitted he'd struggled in other jobs because of his autism, was exactly the kind of conscientious, careful employee she needed. "I couldn't get along without him. Especially not with what I've got coming up." She patted her belly.

"You're going to be such a fantastic mom. I've felt terrible ever since I had to turn you down for that loan, but I guess things worked out in the end."

"They worked out exactly as they were meant to." Meredith squeezed Zach's hand. If she'd gotten that loan, she might never have met with Zach for business advice, might never have married him.

The hostess turned to them expectantly, and Ellen waved and scurried away.

Meredith, Hailey, and Zach followed the hostess to a large table with a sign that said *Reserved.*

Meredith stopped. "Oh, this is bigger than we need. I'd hate to take it when you're so busy."

The hostess waved a hand toward the table. "This is where Ava told me to seat you."

"We may have some surprise guests joining us," Zach said.

"Really?" Meredith nudged him. "Who?"

"We were told to keep that quiet." He winked at Hailey.

Meredith looked from one to the other and shrugged. She knew she'd never get it out of them. She was about to sit when Zach caught her arm. "We should say hello to that table over there."

Meredith put down her purse and pashmina and followed him and Hailey to a long table where Zach's dad sat with Stacey, her husband, Earl Ray, and the rest of the Hamlin family.

She waved to Zach's dad, Stacey, and Earl Ray, and to each of the other couples—Jack and Tess, Becky and Seth,

Abby and Nate, Kristen and Clay, Samantha and Lucas—and to Hank, who she knew from the hardware store. He was still single, a problem that his female cousins had long thought needed to be remedied.

Meredith and Zach chatted a moment, and then she thanked them all for coming to opening night. "So nice to see you all. I hope you enjoy your meal." She turned back to their own table—

And nearly stumbled.

Aunt Ruby, Uncle Harris, Cousin Jake, and his wife, Rita, all stood grinning at her. Jake and Rita's toddler surveyed the room from a wooden highchair, fascinated with the lights hanging from the ceiling.

"Oh, my goodness! You're the surprise!" Meredith rushed toward them.

"We had to be here for opening night," Aunt Ruby said.

Jake waved a hand toward the room. "This place is awesome."

"Just lovely," Rita said.

Uncle Harris pulled Meredith into his arms. "Ruby and I are so proud of you and Ava."

For a second, Meredith gazed at him. Who was this man? He had the same hair and the same build as her uncle, but his eyes shone with a happiness she hadn't seen in decades, and his voice rang with warmth.

"Retirement certainly agrees with you, Uncle Harris."

"It does indeed. So does being a grandpa. The more time I've spent with my granddaughter, the more I've realized what really matters." He squeezed her shoulder. "I'm sorry about how I acted after your folks died. I was wrong to have blamed you. I love you, Meredith, and I hope you can forgive me."

A weight lifted from her frame, and tears hovered on her lashes. "I love you too, Uncle Harris. Of course, I forgive you." She blinked and was wrapped in his hug, and then Aunt Ruby put her arms around both of them.

After a moment, Meredith stepped back and moved over to say hello to Rita, and Zach joined the men, who quickly fell into a deep discussion about the acreage he had purchased.

Uncle Harris wanted details on the placement of the solar panels, and Jake wanted to hear about the jobs the solar farm had brought to Abundance. Zach stood tall as he explained that the project was producing even more energy than they'd hoped. One big investor who joined the project after Joe Webster backed out had been so enthusiastic that Zach and Cliff were putting another solar farm in the county next year. Zach had even installed a small bank of solar collectors behind Meredith's greenhouses, which significantly reduced her electrical costs and should pay for themselves in seven years.

"Were you surprised to see who joined your table?" Ava, every inch the professional in her chef's uniform, appeared behind Aunt Ruby.

"I was." Meredith took her sister's arm, looked her in the eye, and spoke as solemnly as she could. "And I am so very, very proud of you."

Ava pulled her close. "I couldn't have done it without you, sis. This place really should be named Ava and Meredith's."

"That's a bit of a mouthful. Besides, the restaurant was

your dream." A dream that Ava had been eager to pursue again once Meredith explained how she had finally let go of her guilt.

"It might have been my dream," Ava said, "but you helped pay for culinary school, and Zach set up the financing. I'm still amazed that his former in-laws wanted to invest in my business as a show of how they welcomed you to the family."

"Me too, and Zach was shocked. He said it had to be a God thing."

"I need to get back to the kitchen, but I had to tell you that this night is"—Ava fluttered her hands as if reaching for the right words—"even better than I imagined." She turned first one way, then the other, eyes wide, as if the restaurant still overwhelmed her. "Plus, the produce you sent over is gorgeous. With ingredients that good, my job is easy."

Warmth filled Meredith's heart. "Mom and Dad would have been so proud of you."

Ava's eyes shone. "And you too."

"Ava! Meredith!" The man's voice from behind her was familiar, but somehow it didn't fit in Abundance.

Meredith turned and found Marcus walking toward her.

"Your sister is a genius. I should have kept her at The Table and never encouraged her to go to culinary school."

Ava chuckled, but her chest swelled. "He's one of the investors," she whispered to Meredith. "He didn't want me to know until tonight."

"Ah, yes." Marcus nodded as if he'd overheard. "Both of my restaurants have more business than we can handle.

I decided the only way to expand was to invest in other chefs who had real talent. Between your lovely produce and Ava's recipes and skill, I have no doubt this place will be a tremendous success. Just wait until you taste the—"

A sharp pang shot through Meredith's abdomen, and her breath caught.

"Meredith?" Zach rushed to her side.

She laid a hand on his arm. "My back has been hurting all day. I was so busy thinking about the grand opening that I didn't realize what was going on."

"You're in labor?" His eyes grew wide.

"I think so."

"Then we're not taking any chances. We're headed straight to the hospital." He slid an arm around her waist. "Sorry, everyone, it's time for my beautiful bride to become a mom."

She looked at her family and then at Marcus. "I guess I won't get to visit with you all or taste anything. At least not tonight."

"I imagine you've got some pull with the chef," he said. "You can probably get a table here any night of the week."

"Don't worry about us. We're here for the whole weekend." Aunt Ruby's eyes sparkled. "This just means we'll get to see your baby before we go back."

Zach gently sat on the edge of the hospital bed, unable to take his eyes off Meredith holding his son.

His perfect, healthy son.

Emotion swelled in his chest, and pinpricks jabbed at the back of his eyes. With a shaking hand, he brushed a finger across one of the baby's miniature fists and tapped the tip of his tiny nose.

Meredith's face glowed and her eyes radiated joy as she held the sleeping baby with such tenderness that Zach's heart ached.

"Congratulations, Mom," he whispered. "You did it."

"I can't believe it's real." She let out a sigh. "I'm married to you. I get to be a mom to Hailey. And now we have a son."

"I know. It's as if God blessed us with more than I can comprehend." Zach shook his head. "When Hailey and I moved to Abundance, I thought I had everything I ever needed. I had no idea how much I needed to learn to forgive, how much I needed to learn to trust, and how much I needed healing."

But he had. From that moment—when he'd forgiven both Meredith and Jillian and had a long conversation with God—his heart had felt so much lighter.

He brushed a hand over the baby's shoulder. "And I had no idea how much both Hailey and I needed you."

Meredith caught his hand in hers. "I needed you too, so that I could learn to accept forgiveness. So that you could fill my life with love. And so that we could become a family." She peeked down at the little one, then looked back up at him. "It really does seem like God brought us together for a purpose. Like ours was a love meant to be."

Zach nodded.

Meredith stretched her arms toward him. "Would you like to hold him?"

Unable to speak, he carefully took the baby in his arms. His heart felt as if it might burst. No matter how many solar projects he put in, no matter how well his business did, parenting Hailey had been the most rewarding experience of his life. Raising this little boy would be just as amazing. He pressed a kiss, a promise to be the best dad he could, to his son's forehead.

Then he positioned the baby in his left arm and slid his right arm around Meredith's shoulders. "Hailey and the rest of the family want to come in and meet him, but I think first we should give him a name."

"I agree." Meredith looked at the baby's face, then up at him. "Which name do you like? We've discussed so many that I can't pick a favorite."

"I like the one we talked about last night. Bennett."

"It's perfect." Her eyes shone. "Bennett, which means 'blessing.'"

"He is. He most certainly is." As Zach's chest swelled, he smiled down at his son and pulled her closer.

God had been so incredibly generous. His darling Hailey. His wonderful, sweet wife, Meredith. And now his son, Bennett.

God was so good. So very, very good.

A Note from the Author

Dear Reader,

Thank you so much for reading *Love Meant to Be*. I cannot tell you what a joy it is for me to be an author and how grateful I am to every person who reads my stories. I hope this book brought you a smile, and I hope it reminded you how very much God loves you!

In this story, young Hailey deals with some serious issues in Phoenix—bullying and what could be diagnosed as depression. Please know that, although I was able to magically solve them by having her move to Abundance, I know that in real life things aren't that easy. I asked a friend who is a clinical psychologist, and she says that www.psychologytoday.com lists licensed therapists, teletherapy, psychiatrists, and treatment centers by location. In addition, if you know of someone expressing an imminent threat of self-harm, she says you can call the National Suicide Prevention Lifeline at 1-800-273-TALK (8255) or your local emergency room.

Also, I hope this book will remind you to check the batteries in your carbon monoxide detector or, if you don't have one, to get one at your local hardware store. You can buy one for about $20. According to the Centers for Disease Control, about 50,000 people are sent to the emergency room each year due to accidental carbon monoxide poisoning. I don't want one of them to be you, dear reader!

On a happier note, I offer a free copy of my holiday

novella, *Christmas in Abundance,* to anyone who signs up for my author newsletter. It's a sweet, stand-alone story set in the same town as *Love Meant to Be.* I think you'll enjoy it, and I'd love to keep in touch! You can sign up at http://www.sallybayless.com/free-novella/.

If you enjoyed this book, I'd be really grateful if you would write a review on Amazon or Goodreads. Those reviews are the best advertising around, and you wouldn't believe how fun it is to get feedback!

Last but not least, I love to hear from readers! If you'd like to say hello, please email me at author@sallybayless.com or visit my website, where you can find all my social media links.

May God bless you,

Sally Bayless
www.sallybayless.com

ACKNOWLEDGMENTS

I am incredibly grateful to the people who help me as an author. I could not create my books without their generous contributions of time, talent, and knowledge. Any errors that slipped in despite their best efforts are my own.

First, thank you to the experts who helped me make this story more realistic and believable. My critique partner Tammy Doherty not only is a wonderful storyteller, she also runs a greenhouse. Her input on the details about plants, greenhouse construction, and the life of a greenhouse owner was invaluable! Robert A. Holm, Jr., D.O. FACEP, who has helped me with so many of my books, once again reviewed the medical issues in this story. Thank you so much, Tammy and Bob!

Both Tammy and my other critique partner, Susan Anne Mason, helped make this book a much better read with their suggestions on wording and story. Thank you both! Whether it's a grammar question, a massive plot problem, or my never-ending struggle with finding good titles, you two come to the rescue.

My beta readers—Betsy Anderson, Janice Huwe, Kim Mather, Leisa Ostermann, Carrie Saunders, and Stephanie Smith—are such a blessing! Thank you all for your careful reading, your insightful questions, and your great suggestions. Your help and encouragement mean so much!

This book was edited by Christina Tarabochia. Christina, you have such an incredible talent for small, deft edits that make a story shine, while never changing the author's voice. Add in your kind, teaching manner of editing, and I count myself so very lucky to have found you!

The cover of *Love Meant to Be* was designed by Jenny Zemanek of Seedlings Design Studio. Thank you, Jenny, for making my book beautiful and for being such a joy to work with!

To my family, Dave, Michael, and Laurel, thank you for your tech help, your encouragement, and your hugs. A special thanks to Dave for helping me understand solar power generation and transmission. Also, thank you all for your kind understanding that even though you really, really want me to include Sasquatch and velociraptors in one of my books, I have yet to fit them into a Christian romance. One day, maybe... (Maybe not!)

Finally, thank you to Jesus, the author of my joy and salvation.

About the Author

After many years away, Sally Bayless now lives in her hometown in the Missouri Ozarks. She's married and has two grown children. When not working on her next book, she enjoys reading, watching BBC television with her husband, doing Bible studies, swimming, and shopping for cute shoes.

Have you read the prequel to
The Abundance Series?

If not, please turn the page to read the beginning of

Love of a Lifetime

Chapter One

Monday, Aug. 4, 1980

Fear can really do a person in.

Oh, a little caution—the kind that makes a driver keep both eyes on the road—is a good thing.

But too much fear can ruin a person's life.

And starting today, at age twenty-seven, Cara Smith was building a new life, trying to put fear behind her and become the person she wanted to be.

Driving along the rural Missouri highway, she passed a sign for Abundance—the town where she'd chosen to begin that new life—and she attempted to push the pesky tickle of fear away. Then she took another look, noticing a green Lincoln Continental sprawled on the edge of the road.

A woman in a red business suit stood by the raised hood of the vehicle, waving her arms.

The smart thing to do, the cautious thing to do, since Cara was traveling alone, was to stop at the next gas station and ask the attendant to call the highway patrol.

But something about the woman radiated small-town propriety. Slightly frazzled small-town propriety, but propriety nonetheless. And she had two little kids in her backseat.

Cara eased her foot onto the brake. Being smart and cautious was one thing. Being downright unhelpful was another. Besides, wasn't her new life all about being brave? She pulled her white Volare onto the shoulder and turned off the engine.

The woman from the Lincoln hurried to Cara's passenger-side door. She looked about sixty, and her face shone with perspiration. Her hair, which probably began the day with a thick layer of Final Net, drooped on one side. Clearly, she'd chosen that red suit with its formidable shoulder pads because she'd believed she'd spend this sticky August day in air conditioning, not on the side of the road.

Cara reached across the passenger seat and cranked down the window.

"Thanks for stopping," the woman said. "Could you send someone to help? Or give my granddaughters and me a ride into town?" She gestured to the back seat of her car, where two girls who appeared to be identical twins peered out.

"What do you think is wrong?"

"I have no idea. It just died." She glared at the Lincoln, then looked back at Cara. "I'm Imogene Findley, by the way, the mayor of Abundance, that little town up ahead."

"Pleased to meet you. I'm An—uh—Cara Smith." Cara gave a quick smile, hopefully covering her slip, then glanced once more toward the Lincoln. "I'll gladly give you a lift, but I'd like to look at your car first. I'm pretty good with engines."

"If you think you can fix it, please, go ahead," Imogene said, but skepticism flickered across her eyes.

For a female mayor, Imogene didn't seem very confident in the abilities of a woman. And she should be. It was 1980 after all.

Granted, Cara wasn't a professional mechanic. But when a girl was raised by a father on his own, a somewhat distant father at that, then a shared understanding of engines became a way to connect. And, as she'd learned when she grew older, a knowledge of machinery was a handy thing to have.

Behind Imogene, one of the little girls waved from the back seat, her brown pigtails bouncing.

Cara waved back, waited until a pickup truck passed, and climbed out of her Volare. "If I can't take care of it in ten minutes, I'll drive you into town."

"Thanks. That would be great." Imogene gestured to her car. "I'm going to get back in to keep an eye on the girls."

Cara nodded, dug through the emergency supplies in her trunk for a rag, then went to the front of the Lincoln and studied the engine. A lock of hair—red hair—that had escaped her ponytail fell forward, and she pushed it behind her ear. A new hair color, a new name... The changes still tripped her up. If she was going to keep her identity a secret, she needed to get used to her new self. Fast.

For now, she should focus on this engine. Was it the radiator? Using the rag to protect her hand from the heat, she checked. No. Were the spark plug cables connected? She jiggled them. They felt fine. Wait a minute…

"You've got a broken battery cable," she called out.

Humph. She could replace the cable, but she didn't have one handy. She walked back to Imogene's window, mentally running through the contents of her Volare. Which would be…well, everything she owned. But what did she have that was useful and easily accessible?

"I'm kind of ashamed to admit this," Imogene said, "but I don't know how serious a problem that is. Before my husband died three years ago, I didn't even know how to put gas in the car."

Cara kept her expression neutral. That explained the woman's skepticism about Cara's car-repair skills. "A broken battery cable isn't too serious." She hesitated. "You know how to fill your tank now, right?"

"I sure do," Imogene said. "I've learned a lot since Harold died. And I got elected."

"Then I'd say you've been very resilient."

"Thank you." The older woman sat up taller. "It took me a while."

"That's understandable after such a loss," Cara said. Emotional trauma was hard to get past. She should know. But she had a plan for her own resilience, a plan that included moving to Abundance, a town she'd never heard of before last week and picked solely because of its name. Surely things would *have* to be better in a place called Abundance. With a new town, a new look, and a new name, she could start over and find what she so desperately wanted—a community, possibly even one day a family, to make her feel valued and loved.

But first, this repair job. "Is that your briefcase?" She pointed to the seat beside Imogene.

"Ye-es," Imogene said, sounding as if she now had more doubts about Cara's roadside assistance.

"Sorry, dumb question." What else could the big black case be? "What I mean is, do you have any binder clips in there?"

A grin spread across Imogene's face. "What size do you need?"

Two minutes later, Cara yelled out from under the hood. "Try it now."

Imogene cranked the engine, and it roared to life.

Cara hooked her thumbs in her shorts pockets and gave the engine a nod of approval. She'd done it! Who said a woman couldn't have a little mechanical know-how? She used the rag to protect her fingers as she lowered the sunbaked hood, then went to talk to Imogene.

"I can't believe you fixed it," Imogene said with a note of respect. "With office supplies."

"It might hold quite a while, but you should get a new cable as soon as you can. How about I follow you into town just in case? I'm headed there anyway to pick up the key to my apartment."

Imogene's head angled to one side. "Are you new to Abundance?"

"I am. I'm moving in today, and tomorrow I begin looking for a job."

"What do you do? Maybe I can help."

"Usually accounting, but I'd take any office position.

I'm a decent typist." She was also skilled at dodging reporters, but there was no need to mention that. "And I'm rather good at dealing with copiers that act up."

"I bet you are." Imogene looked Cara up and down. "I've been having a terrible time hiring a new secretary. Why don't you come in tomorrow for an interview?"

The air whooshed out of Cara's lungs. A possible job, just because she'd stopped to help? "Really? That would be great."

"Nine o'clock." Imogene reached out the window and gave Cara a firm handshake. "This may work out well. You're clearly bright, and if you can do battle with that copier the way you dealt with this car, all of city hall will thank me. Let me give you directions to my office."

Will Hamlin glanced from the highway to the notebook on the passenger seat of his Toyota pickup. He'd had an excellent interview with Alice Butler, a retired school-bus driver. That interview would make a solid feature story, the type of feature that he, as the new editor, wanted more of in *The Abundance News*.

Of course, Alice hadn't thought Abundance needed to know how she quietly helped the homebound elderly, but Will did. Once he mentioned that a story about her kindness might inspire someone else to think of others, she'd agreed to the interview.

Each week, Alice stopped by the homes of thirteen people, each too old or frail to drive, each of whom lived alone. She visited, she said, to make sure their glasses were clean. "Folks who are far-sighted can't see very well when they take their glasses off to wash them, but I can see every one of those spots."

But Alice did more than merely polish the glasses of the people she visited. She asked about their health, made sure their prescriptions were filled, and checked that food was in the fridge. Most importantly, for many of the people she visited, Alice was the only person they saw each week.

It wasn't a job. She wasn't paid by the county or the state or the federal government. She did it because she hoped someone would do the same for her when she was older. "And," she said, "because it's the Christian thing to do."

The humility of the woman, the basic goodness—that was what Will wanted to capture in his article.

Once he got back to the paper, he'd do his best. Then he would go home, take off his tie, and change out of his dress shirt and pants and into some gym shorts. He would have a nice, quiet evening with no meeting to cover. He might even take his TV dinner out on his back deck. He was actually supposed to have Mondays off since he worked every Saturday getting out both the Saturday and Sunday editions. Being promoted from reporter to editor hadn't meant much of a shift in his job duties, just the addition of more.

But what was going on up ahead?

Two cars sat at the side of the road, a green Lincoln Continental with an Abundance Lions Club bumper sticker and a white Volare. The Volare was unfamiliar and probably belonged to that redheaded woman. But the Lincoln? That belonged to Imogene Findley, the mayor who was furious with him.

Had they been in a wreck? He couldn't tell from here. Whatever was going on, it appeared Imogene was in trouble. Will pulled up behind her car and climbed out. He might be able to help her and by doing so get back in her good graces. She was an important news source. He needed her to take his calls. And besides, most of the time they got along well. After all, they both loved Abundance.

He looked more closely at the redhead. Mid-twenties. Wearing tan shorts and a pale blue T-shirt. Evidently, she was someone passing through. Any girl that cute in his hometown, he would have noticed.

He walked over to where she stood by Imogene's window.

Imogene's granddaughters waved frantically from the backseat as if they were afraid he might not notice them.

He bent down and peeked in. "Hey, girls. Nice blue hair ribbons, Joanna. And Jennifer, I like your purple ones."

Jennifer patted her pigtails, and Joanna's eyes sparkled.

He stood back up and looked at Imogene and the redhead. "Hi, Imogene. And—"

"If it isn't Will Hamlin, my least favorite person." Imogene held out a hand toward the redhead. "Will, meet Cara Smith. She's just moving to Abundance."

"Nice to meet you," he said. He shot a look at Imogene. Not the most gracious introduction he'd ever had.

"Pleased to meet you too." Cara reached to shake his hand but stopped. She wiped her fingers on a rag she held, then waved and tucked her hands behind her.

Up close, she looked even prettier. Her eyes were a pale greenish-blue, the sort of eyes a man might drown in, like the sea by some Mediterranean island.

And she was moving to Abundance? Wow. Lately, it seemed women his age only wanted to leave.

"Will's the editor of the local paper, *The Abundance News*," Imogene said to Cara. "A publication that doesn't always quote people correctly. Something to remember if you work with him professionally."

Cara's shoulders stiffened, and she took a half step back.

Heat flared in Will's chest. "Imogene, you know that misquote was in an article written by your niece, the same niece you asked me to hire as an intern this summer."

"Who I expect you to be training up better than that. I've been working for months to bring that manufacturer to Abundance. Cyndi's article may have blown our chance. The community needs those jobs."

"I'm having her personally mail them a copy of the retraction," Will said. "There's not much more I can do."

Imogene's mouth pinched up.

He shrugged. He was trying his best as editor, although some days he wondered if, at thirty, he was ready for the challenge. Obviously, Cyndi hadn't been ready for hers. He'd given her a chance with that big story, but she'd gotten the main quote of the piece all wrong. Unfortunately, he had no way of knowing until after the story ran, when the source called to complain. For now, she was back to writing the police reports, community calendar, and obits. "Anyway, I saw you two on the side of the road here. Do you need help?"

"Can you fix a broken battery cable?" Imogene's voice had a condescending note.

"Well, no." To be honest, he didn't know how to fix anything. Except a run-on sentence. "But I can offer you a ride to town."

"Not necessary," Imogene said. "Cara fixed it. No need to assume we're helpless just because we're female."

Will tugged at his collar. He hadn't made any such assumption. "I was simply trying to help."

The two women looked at him with the same expression, like royalty dismissing riffraff.

He turned and walked back to his truck. If he'd had any sense, he'd have driven by and stayed in the air conditioning.

Stopping had been a waste of time, time he should have spent on his feature.

And clearly, he'd never have a shot with that cute redhead. The mayor had already convinced her that he was an irresponsible journalist and sexist to boot.

Thanks a lot, Imogene.

All of Sally's books are available in e-book and paperback from Amazon.

Sign up for Sally's newsletter at www.sallybayless.com and get a link to download the holiday novella *Christmas in Abundance* for free in ebook or PDF!